Samuel French Acting Edition

The Workroom (L'Atelier)

by Jean-Claude Grumberg

Translated by
Daniel A. Stein with Sara O'Connor

SAMUELFRENCH.COM   SAMUELFRENCH.CO.UK

ISBN 978-0-573-61826-0

www.SamuelFrench.com
www.SamuelFrench.co.uk

FOR PRODUCTION ENQUIRIES

UNITED STATES AND CANADA
Info@SamuelFrench.com
1-866-598-8449

UNITED KINGDOM AND EUROPE
Plays@SamuelFrench.co.uk
020-7255-4302

Each title is subject to availability from Samuel French, depending upon
country of performance. Please be aware that *THE WORKROOM* may
not be licensed by Samuel French in your territory. Professional and
amateur producers should contact the nearest Samuel French office or
licensing partner to verify availability.

---

publisher. No one shall upload this title(s), or part of this title(s), to any social media websites.

For all enquiries regarding motion picture, television, and other media rights, please contact Samuel French.

MUSIC USE NOTE

Licensees are solely responsible for obtaining formal written permission from copyright owners to use copyrighted music in the performance of this play and are strongly cautioned to do so. If no such permission is obtained by the licensee, then the licensee must use only original music that the licensee owns and controls. Licensees are solely responsible and liable for all music clearances and shall indemnify the copyright owners of the play(s) and their licensing agent, Samuel French, against any costs, expenses, losses and liabilities arising from the use of music by licensees. Please contact the appropriate music licensing authority in your territory for the rights to any incidental music.

IMPORTANT BILLING AND CREDIT REQUIREMENTS

If you have obtained performance rights to this title, please refer to your licensing agreement for important billing and credit requirements.

THE WORKROOM was first presented in the U.S. by the Milwaukee Repertory Theater on March 7, 1980. The production was directed by John Dillon, Settings by David Emmons, Costumes by Patricia McGourty, Lighting by Arden Fingerhut, Properties by Sandy Struth, Production Stage Manager, Robert Goodman.

The cast in order of speaking was as follows:

Helene	Maggie Burke
Simone	Peggy Cowles
Gisele	Julie Garfield
Mme. Laurence	Marge Kotlisky
Marie	Dana Barton
Mimi	Rose Pickering
Leon	William Leach
First Presser	Larry Shue
Machine Operators	Henry Burko
	Rick Weber
Jean, Second Presser	Jack McLaughlin-Gary
Max	George Axler
Boy	Matthew Knuth

PLACE: Paris after World War II

SOUTH STREET THEATRE

424 West 42nd Street
On Theatre Row, NYC

AMERICAN THEATRE ALLIANCE
under the direction of Aaron Levin and Jerold Barnard
presents
JEAN-CLAUDE GRUMBERG'S
THE WORKROOM
(L'ATELIER)
American Version by
DANIEL A. STEIN
with SARA O'CONNOR
with
(in alphabetical order)
RICHARD COSTABILE
MARGARET DULANEY
RITA GARDNER
ELAINE GROLLMAN
MICHAEL GUIDO
BEN R. KELMAN
ROBIN LEARY
FRANK MARADEN
JUNE SQUIBB
MARK STEFAN
EUGENE TROOBNICK
CARRIE ZIVETZ

Scenery by	*Lighting by*	*Costumes by*
JOHN KASARDA	ROBBY MONK	RICHARD HORNUNG

&
VIVIEN LEONE

Casting by	*Production Stage Manager*
MAUREEN SNELLING	MELANIE HULSE

Dance Sequence Choreographed by
ISABEL GLASSER
Directed by
AARON LEVIN
An Equity Approved Funded Non-Profit Theatre Code Production

THE CHARACTERS
(in order of appearance)

Helene..........................RITA GARDNER
Simone....................MARGARET DULANEY
Gisele..............................JUNE SQUIBB
Marie..............................ROBIN LEARY
Madame Laurence ....ELAINE GROLLMAN
Mimi...........................CARRIE ZIVETZ
Leon......................EUGENE TROOBNICK
First Presser...................FRANK MARADEN
Machine Operator..........RICHARD COSTABILE
Jean ....MICHAEL GUIDO
Max...........................BEN R. KELMAN
the Boy.........................MARK STEFAN

PLACE: A tailoring workroom in Paris.

THERE WILL BE ONE INTERMISSION.
IT OCCURS AFTER SCENE 5.

A tailoring workroom in Paris. There are two small tables. The women perch on stools next to the table which is by the window. There is also a cutting table and a third table for the PRESSER. There are two entrances: one leads off to the stairs; the other leads to LEON'S apartment. A small spool table is optional.

Scene 1

THE TRY-OUT

Very early morning, 1945. SIMONE sits at the table, working. Standing near another table — HELENE, the owner's wife, also works. From time to time she glances at SIMONE.

HELENE. In 1943 they took my sister, as well....

SIMONE. Has she come back?

HELENE. No ... she was twenty-two. *(silence)* You worked for yourself?

SIMONE. Yes, just my husband and me; during the busy season we took on a worker.... I had to sell the machine last month; he won't even be able to go back to work.... I shouldn't have sold it, but....

HELENE. You can always find a machine....

SIMONE. *(Nods in agreement.)* I shouldn't have sold it.... Someone offered me some coal and.... *(silence)*

HELENE. You have children?

SIMONE. Yes, two boys....

HELENE. How old?

SIMONE. Ten and six....

HELENE. Spaced just about right ... at least that's what they say.... I don't have children.

(GISELE enters.)

SIMONE. They get along very well. The older one takes care of the younger. During the occupation we sent them to the free zone; when they came back the big boy had to explain to the little one who I was. The little one hid behind his big brother, he didn't want to see me; he called me "Madame"....

HELENE. Without children you often wonder what you're here for....

SIMONE. It's not too late.... *(GISELE, at the coatrack, takes off her jacket, hangs it up, puts on her smock and takes her place. With a nod, she greets SIMONE and MME. HELENE.)*

HELENE. *(Introduces SIMONE.)* Madame Gisele ... Madame Simone; here for finishing work. *(SIMONE and GISELE nod and smile to each other.)*

(GISELE is already at work as MME. LAURENCE enters, closely followed by MARIE. They both greet MME. HELENE.)

MME. LAURENCE and MARIE. Bonjour Madame Helene. *(They change into their smocks. MARIE finishes buttoning hers while already beginning her first piece. MME. LAURENCE takes her time — even takes off her shoes, which she swaps for slippers. Shuffling her feet, she goes to her place at the end of the table facing SIMONE, with her back to the window on a high stool. Thus, she dominates the situation. HELENE, standing in front of her table, bastes the cloth onto the front of the jacket while glancing at the others from time to time.)*

(MIMI, coughing, enters hurriedly and is acknowledged by HELENE.)

GISELE. Did you fall out of bed again this morning? *(MIMI, putting on her blouse, gestures as if to say: "Don't talk to me about it.")*

HELENE. *(Introduces her.)* Madame Simone ... Madame Laurence, Mademoiselle Marie, Mademoiselle Mimi. *(SIMONE smiles at them.)*

MME. LAURENCE. *(As soon as MIMI begins to crowd MME. LAURENCE with her work, MME LAURENCE backs her stool away slightly and speaks to her.)* Someday you're going to put my eye out.... *(MIMI disregards this and works in silence. GISELE hums mechanically.)*

HELENE. Things are going well today, Madame Gisele!

GISELE. *(surprised)* For Me? No, why?

HELENE. Since I hear you humming....

GISELE. I'm not humming, Madame Helene; I don't have the heart for it. Especially not these days.... *(MARIE and MIMI join in on "not these days" and burst out laughing together.)*

MME. LAURENCE. *(after glancing at SIMONE'S work)* You did finishing work? *(SIMONE agrees.)* It shows; you make pretty little stitches....

(The owner, M. LEON, suddenly pops his head inside the door and shouts loudly.)

LEON. Helene, Helene! *(All the workers are startled; they let out a squeal and then burst into laughter. HELENE sighs. LEON can be heard getting annoyed in the other room — perhaps on the telephone. SIMONE, who had been as startled as everyone else, laughs heartily. MME. HELENE goes out and shuts the door behind her. She and her husband can be heard talking as they move away from the closed door.)*

GISELE. We're off to a fine start.... If he's yelling this early in the morning....

MME. LAURENCE. There's trouble brewing....

SIMONE. Is he always like that?

MME. LAURENCE. Monsieur Leon? You haven't seen him yet? We'll let it be a surprise.

MIMI. *(in a very hoarse voice, nearly voiceless)* He'll hear about this.

MME. LAURENCE. What?

MIMI. He's going to hear about this.

MME. LAURENCE. What?!

MIMI. *(Still hoarse; she'll speak this way until the end of the scene.)* I'm going to repeat that to him.

MME. LAURENCE. *(taking the others as witnesses)* That's not fair. She's crazy, the little slut. What did I say? What did I say? *(MIMI clears her throat without answering. MARIE chokes back laughter. MME LAURENCE crushes her with a glance.)* You find that funny?

MARIE. It's her voice.... *(She bursts out laughing. To*

MIMI:) It's your voice.

MIMI. *(after coughing furiously)* This is funny? You don't give a damn about my sore throat? *(MARIE nods her head.)* People's misery has always amused imbeciles....

MARIE. *(laughing)* Thank you.

GISELE. Nowadays you've got to laugh; it's a substitute for meat. *(MIMI coughs.)*

SIMONE. *(Looks in her purse and finds a box of cough drops which she offers.)* They're good for the throat...

MIMI. *(taking one)* Thanks.... *(SIMONE offers some to the others, who accept them.)*

MARIE. *(reads)* "Pectoides: candy cough drops, soothe the throat, sweeten and refresh the breath."

GISELE. *(to SIMONE)* You can tell who has children.... *(SIMONE nods in agreement.)* How many?

SIMONE. Two.

GISELE. It's a tough job, isn't it?

MIMI. Why don't you ever offer us candy? You're a mother, aren't you?

GISELE. I don't even give them to my kids; would you like me to buy some expressly for you?

MIMI. As a matter of fact, I would. You never offer us anything.... *(GISELE stays quiet.)*

MME. LAURENCE. *(to MIMI)* You'd be smart to avoid talking today. Give your voice a rest for a change.... *(MIMI snickers and her voice quavers.)* It's for your own good, isn't it? Of course if you think that what you have to say is important.... *(Brief silence, she continues.)* Even so, a day of silence would be a blessing. *(MIMI has a coughing fit; she ends up aiming it at MME. LAURENCE, who pulls back slightly and then, dignified.)* Would it trouble you too much to allow me a little breathing space?

GISELE and MARIE. *(together)* My dear....

MIMI. What? What's she talking about? *(MME LAU-RENCE puts down the piece she's just finished, rises and goes out. MIMI is trying to speak in an undertone.)* The bathroom brigade is starting earlier than usual; she needs a plumber to cork that up.... *(Her voice gives out, she clears her throat and coughs. SIMONE takes out her cough drops but MIMI refuses with a gesture.)*

GISELE. *(to SIMONE)* You'd do better to save them for your kids.

MARIE. How did you catch that?

MIMI. *(shrugging)* I don't know .... I went dancing last night; coming out I got soaked.

GISELE. Did it rain last night?

MIMI. *(shaking her head "no")* I fell in the gutter. *(MARIE bursts out laughing.)* Go ahead and laugh. I was with Huguette, my friend Huguette....

GISELE. The fat one?

MIMI. She's not so fat.

GISELE. Isn't she the one you called the "big cow"?

MIMI. *(agrees)* Yes, but that doesn't mean she's fat. She's a slob.... Yesterday we went to the dance hall together. I took off my shoes to dance and at the end I couldn't find them again.... *(MARIE is doubled up with laughter. SIMONE begins to chuckle also.)*

GISELE. You lost your shoes?

MIMI. Yeah, somebody lifted them....

GISELE. Since when do you have to take off your shoes to dance?

MIMI. To swing — to dance swing. So these two

Americans sweetly offered to see us home; one carried me so I wouldn't get my tootsies wet and then I don't know what they were jabbering about, but the next thing I knew one of them asked me something — I didn't understand exactly what, but I nodded my head "yes" and my girl-friend did, too, and without warning the guy drops me smack bang into the gutter. I was soaked to the skin and then Huguette and the two Americans start laughing to beat the band, so we get into this big brawl. *(She clears her throat; it hurts more and more.)* This morning I woke up like this; I couldn't talk at all.... *(GISELE, MARIE and SIMONE double up laughing.)*

MME. LAURENCE. *(Returns to her stool and asks:)* Laughing at me again? *(GISELE, MARIE and SIMONE shake their heads "no", laughing even harder. MME LAURENCE addresses SIMONE, who forces herself to stop laughing out of politeness.)* So you've joined them already. It doesn't matter; I'm used to it. She turns everybody against me. *(SIMONE can't control herself; she laughs more and more nervously, constantly excusing herself.)*

GISELE. *(to MME. LAURENCE)* Nobody said anything about you; not a word....

MIMI. *(to GISELE)* Quit it .... it's not nice to lie; especially after what you said... *(SIMONE now has her handkerchief in her hand; she's no longer working, she mops her eyes while continuing to excuse herself at each burst of laughter.)*

MIMI. That's what you get when you don't understand American lingo. Huguette said to me that I shouldn't have nodded "yes".

MARIE. Were they drunk, or what?

GISELE. So you came back all wet and barefooted?

MIMI. *(who laughs now in turn)* My skirt stuck to me everywhere... It had shrunk; real trash this whore of a fiber.... *(They laugh all over again, SIMONE the most. Little by little, calm returns.)*

GISELE. How can you go dancing like that every night?

MIMI. I don't go every night; I went yesterday....

MARIE. Simone, do you go dancing too? *(SIMONE shakes her head "no", laughing.)*

GISELE. She said she has children.

MARIE. It's against the law to go dancing when you have children? *(GISELE, irritated, shakes her head.)* You could even go dancing with your husband, right?

SIMONE. *(simply to cut it short)* These days I don't go dancing.

GISELE. There!

MARIE. But you used to go?

SIMONE. Yes ... from time to time....

MARIE. Your husband's the one who doesn't like it?

SIMONE. He's not here; he was deported.) *(brief silence)*

MIMI. When I think what a skunk that GI was.... I'll bet *he* was the one who pinched my shoes!

GISELE. Brilliant! All you had to do was not take them off.... Honestly I've never—

MIMI. *(cutting her off)* *You* go dancing?

GISELE. Sure.

MIMI. No kidding?

GISELE. When I was a girl....

MIMI. *You* were a girl? No kidding!

GISELE. In any case, I never danced with Army trash....

MARIE. Why not, if they're not German?

GISELE. Just because they're not German doesn't mean they're safe.... *(She turns toward SIMONE.)* I'm sorry to have to say it but sometimes the Americans.... *(She stops.)*

MIMI. *(after a while)* C'mon, spit it out, let's have it all.

MME. LAURENCE. Exactly what is it that you want to say, Madame Gisele?

GISELE. Nothing, nothing.

MME. LAURENCE. *(conciliatory)* You'd rather have the Germans than the Americans?

GISELE. I didn't say that; don't put words in my mouth.

MME. LAURENCE. *(more and more conciliatory)* We're only talking about manners of course.

GISELE. When you put it that way I'd say yes, although it's like everything else: there are two sides....

MIMI. You want someone to ask them back; you miss the Krauts? *(She whistles under her breath. GISELE shrugs her shoulders. Silence.)*

MME. LAURENCE. It's true that as long as the Americans weren't here we prayed for their arrival; now that they're here, we're praying that they go away.

MIMI. Speak for yourself. They don't bother me, except when they snitch my shoes and dump me in the water.

MME. LAURENCE. I find that they lack a bit of....

MARIE. Was there one who lacked respect for *you*, Madame Laurence? *(MIMI shouts with laughter. MME LAURENCE raises her shoulders.)*

(The door opens. HELENE calls.)

HELENE. Madame Simone, come here please. *(SI-MONE rises, puts down her work. HELENE calls from the door.)* No, no, bring it with you. *(HELENE disappears.)*

GISELE. Have you already discussed money? *(SIMONE shakes her head "no".)* You don't have to let yourself get taken, you know....

MARIE. *(whispers)* Watch yourself, his hands are a little bit like a crab's.... *(SIMONE goes out.)*

MME. LAURENCE. *(to MARIE)* What did you say?

MARIE. When?

MME. LAURENCE. You said something about crabs?

MARIE. I said he had hands like a crab.

MME. LAURENCE. *(after a moment)* I don't understand. *(MARIE shrugs. MIMI demonstrates LEON'S "pinching".)*

GISELE. He's a good man anyway.

MARIE. *(irritated)* That doesn't prevent.... *(silence)*

MIMI. *(to MARIE)* She's one.

MARIE. What?

MIMI. *(pointing to SIMONE'S stool)* She's another one.

MARIE. Another what? *(MIMI makes a gesture outlining a hooked nose.)* You're crazy.

MIMI. Really!

MARIE. I don't believe it....

MIMI. I recognize them. I have the knack; I recognize them. *(MARIE shrugs.)*

GISELE. In any case, she's a good person.

MIMI. Oh, la la, as far as she's concerned *everybody's* a good person today....

GISELE. I happen to like her, that's all.

MIMI. I happen to like her, too ... but that doesn't prevent her from being one....

MME. LAURENCE. She has an odd laugh! *(silence)*

GISELE. The poor thing can't have had much chance to laugh recently. Not with all her troubles.

MIMI. So what? Everybody has troubles; I lost my shoes but I don't make it a—

GISELE. *(to MARIE with reproach)* And you go and ask her if her husband likes to dance?

MARIE. How was I to know?

MME. LAURENCE. Some things you can sense....

MARIE. *(Has finished her piece; she looks around for another. She's angry.)* I don't have any more work!

GISELE. Go look for some.

MARIE. *(without getting up)* That's not my job....

GISELE. You prefer to lose a piece rather than move your ass?

MARIE. If I do it this time, I'll always be expected to go get it.... But why don't I have any more work?

(SIMONE has come back and taken her place again.)

GISELE. *(Asks her.)* Well?

SIMONE. Everything's fine ... just fine.

MME. LAURENCE. Did you get everything straight? *(SIMONE doesn't understand.)* You got what you wanted?

SIMONE. Yes, the usual, I guess....

GISELE. You'll see, everything will go well; there's work here year 'round.

MARIE. *(more and more irritated)* There's work *everywhere* these days!

GISELE. Right, there's another reason; here, too.

MIMI. What did you think of our boss—the monkey?

SIMONE. The usual, I guess ... the usual....

MIMI. Start making bigger stitches if you want to get through quickly, you've got to cut corners a little, otherwise....

(HELENE enters.)

HELENE. *(to MIMI)* You're always full of good advice, Mademoiselle Mimi.

MIMI. I didn't hear you come in, Madame Helene. You should wear your wooden-soled shoes for work, and save your rubber ones for Sunday.

MARIE. Madame Helene, I've finished my piece and....

(LEON enters; he's very nervous.)

LEON. *(to HELENE)* So, have you told them?

HELENE. No, I'm getting there....

LEON. So what are you waiting for?

HELENE. *(sighs)* I've come to tell them, I'm getting there, all right....

GISELE. What's up, Monsieur Leon?

LEON. She's going to tell you, she's going to tell you.... *(He goes out.)*

HELENE. *(calling him)* Since you're here already, tell them yourself.

LEON. *(from the other room)* If I tell you to tell them, I don't want you to tell me "You tell them"....

HELENE. *(addressing the workers, while busily moving about the workshop)* We didn't receive the fabric they were sup-

posed to deliver so Monsieur Leon hasn't been able to cut
... the machine operators are going home. So, in short,
finish what you're working on and go home.

MARIE.   What? *(HELENE is already outside.)* What did she
say?

GISELE.   Wonderful! Now what do I do to kill the
afternoon?

MIMI.   You can hurry back home to your dear little
man....

GISELE.   If you think that's funny....

MARIE.   Do you see: he doesn't receive his fabric and
we're the ones left in the lurch; he doesn't give a damn if
we come for nothing. I travelled all the way across Paris.
"Go home!" They're so organized, it's scary....

MME. LAURENCE.   It's all the same to me, mesdames.
*(She gets up, puts her scissors in her box and begins to exit. MARIE
and MIMI go out. GISELE and SIMONE remain seated; they
finish their work in silence.)*

Scene 2

SONGS

A little before noon in 1946. All the workers are present. The PRESSER is at his ironing table. GISELE has a headache and is choking on a pill.

MIMI. What's the matter with you?

GISELE. I've a headache.

SIMONE. It's a long way from the feet. *(GISELE tries to get down her pill. She tries many times.)*

MIMI. Can't you get it down? *(GISELE shakes her head "no" and takes another swallow of water.)* Her hole's too small. *(MARIE laughs.)*

GISELE. *(to MARIE)* C'mon ... do me a favor....

MARIE. A person can't laugh anymore?

GISELE. Not all the time.

MARIE. With you around, it averages out.

GISELE. I'd like to see you take it. *(She goes back to work.)*

MIMI. Just don't think about it anymore....

GISELE. Don't think about the headache that's killing me?....

MIMI. Sing us something; that will make you feel better. *(They all insist. GISELE shakes her head "no" without answering.)* Shit, you're a pain....

GISELE. I don't feel like singing.

MIMI. C'mon, love, for my sake.

MME. LAURENCE. She likes to make us ask.

GISELE. Fine, *you* sing....

MME. LAURENCE. If I had your gift—

GISELE. Here it comes, the soft soap....

MARIE. *(singing)*

I HAVE TWO GREAT OXEN IN MY STABLE *(speaks)* go on.... *(She picks it up again.)*

TWO GREAT WHITE OXEN.

GISELE. If I had two great oxen I wouldn't be here.... *(pause)* The butchers are going to be closed three days a week....

MME. LAURENCE. Not for everyone; when it's closed out front, it's open around the back.

MIMI. *(Sings.)*

FROM THE FRONT, FROM THE BACK

SADLY AS ALWAYS

SHE'S KNOWN LOVE.

GISELE. *(While MIMI is singing, GISELE continues.)* It's true that for some people there's always plenty.

MME. LAURENCE. *(articulating clearly)* There's plenty ... but not for everyone!

GISELE. You wonder how they do it....

MARIE. Eechh! Can't you talk about other things?

GISELE. I'd like to see you manage....

MARIE. Isn't it just as tough for me?

GISELE. You — you haven't any children!

MARIE. So what? Madame Laurence doesn't .... neither does Mimi.

GISELE. C'mon, it's easy when you're young.... *(brief silence)* Less bread than in '43!

SIMONE. And their bread isn't good....

GISELE. To say nothing about how hard it is to get....

SIMONE. It wasn't good during the war, either.

GISELE. Yes, but at least there was a war on.

MME. LAURENCE. What could I cook on Saturday that would be good and filling?

MIMI. Horse balls.

MME. LAURENCE. For heaven's sake....

MIMI. What's the matter, they're good and they're filling.

MME. LAURENCE. There will be eight of us; my husband is inviting—

MIMI. *(cutting her off)* Then get two pairs. *(silence)*

GISELE. It's true you have your husband....

MME. LAURENCE. What about my husband?

MIMI. Tough to be a policeman, isn't it?

MME. LAURENCE. He has the same rights as everybody ... the same rights. *(GISELE is about to say something, holds back, sighs and goes back to her work. Silence. GISELE continuing to work, her nose stuck close to the jacket, begins to sing mechanically to herself in a soft voice. MIMI alerts the others and then accompanies her in a grotesque manner. GISELE stops abruptly.)*

MIMI. Well, hon? Gisou? What's up?

GISELE. You think I don't notice when you make fun of me?

MIMI. I was just doing the harmony to make it prettier.

GISELE. Thanks. *(They all insist, but GISELE quietly resists.)*

MIMI. Gisele, everyone's going to turn away so as not to disturb you; even the presser is going to turn away. O.K., presser of my heart, turn your head, right? Don't look at the artist; go on turn around, girls, that's it.... *(They all turn around. MIMI continues looking at the presser.)* There, you see, no one is looking at you and I won't add the harmony anymore since you don't like it. *(Silence. They are all turned away. Only GISELE is her habitual place; she seems absolutely opposed to the idea of singing. The workers continue to work, searching gropingly for their scissors or their spools of thread on the table without turning their heads back toward GISELE. Suddenly GISELE starts a very sentimental song, which she sings in a strong voice. MARIE, on her chair, resists as long as she can; soon, little-by-little, laughter overcomes MIMI, MME. LAURENCE, then SIMONE. But already GISELE has stopped in the middle of a note. She now works in silence with ferocious energy.)*

MIMI. Well, why are you stopping?

GISELE. They're making fun of me....

MIMI. Not at all; they were even moved....

GISELE. She, she, she, she's making fun of me. *(MARIE bursts out laughing.)* Because it's not swing, it's not zoot-suit music. *(She sings in a mocking tone.)*

THERE ARE ZOOT-SUITERS IN MY QUARTER, BOUM, TRA LA LA TSOIN TSOIN. *(speaks)* —that's good, that's swell.

MARIE. I didn't say anything to you.

GISELE. As soon as I sing she makes fun of me.... You — all you can do is sing your jitter-bug crap instead of letting other people sing; it's easy to make fun. *(She imitates another "zoot" song in a nasal voice.)*

MARIE. What's the matter with her?

MIMI. Good question. Gisou, what's wrong, did you eat some horsemeat?

GISELE. Everything is going to pot here because of your kind. You no longer give a damn for anything, you screech like something in the zoo, you jerk up and down, you respect nothing, you don't even know how to work....

MARIE. *(to GISELE)* What are you saying?

GISELE. Young girls don't even know how to stitch anymore, that's what I'm saying, and I'm not the only one to say it, believe me....

MARIE. *(half-risen)* Shut-up, shut-up....

GISELE. All right, then, turd, tell me you're not the one who....

MARIE. *(Gets up, throws her piece and shouts.)* Shut-up, I tell you, shut-up! *(GISELE gets up next. MIMI, SIMONE and MME. LAURENCE continue to stitch, all the while trying to hold onto the spools which are rolling about on the table.)*

PRESSER. *(Puts down his iron and tries to joke.)* Fight, murder each other, but whatever you do, don't hurt yourselves....

MARIE. Mind your own business; nobody asked you to butt in.... *(The PRESSER beats a retreat. The sewing machine OPERATORS stick their heads into the door to see what's going on. GISELE gives up first; she drops her work and goes out running past the machine OPERATORS. MARIE lets go of the table and sits back down on her stool.)*

OPERATORS. *(They persist.)* Hey — what's going on?

MIMI. *(Rises. Shouts at them.)* Will you leave us alone, you goons? Nobody needs men here. Nobody's broken into your tents to steal your women. It's incredible, just incredible.... *(The OPERATORS beat a retreat. MARIE suddenly collapses onto the table in tears; she very quickly gets control of herself and soon picks up her work again.)*

MIMI. Beautiful! There's one sniveling in the john and one sniveling here, shit! *(MME. LAURENCE shakes her head disapprovingly and whistles between her teeth.)* Stop it, that annoys me! *(MME. LAURENCE continues without noticing. Silence.)*

SIMONE. There are days when nothing goes right. Even the thread keeps breaking....

MIMI. *(Has finished her piece. She doesn't take another one. She rummages in her basket and finds her lunch box.)* This isn't going to stop my appetite.... Very warm, very Parisian, hmm? *(She hands her lunchbox to the PRESSER.)*

PRESSER. *(Lifts his iron from the gas plate and puts the lunchpail in its place.)* Any more? *(MME. LAURENCE brings hers.)*

MARIE. *(Throws down her work, gets up and leaves, grumbling.)* I'm going out.

MIMI. *(mocking)* Oh well....

MME. LAURENCE. *(to SIMONE)* You're still not bringing anything warm?

SIMONE. I didn't have the time to fix it.

MME. LAURENCE. You didn't have the heart, I understand.

MIMI. You've got to eat shit .... otherwise....

MME. LAURENCE. You've got to eat some meat! *(MIMI and MME. LAURENCE put their semblance of a table setting on the corner of a table. Having finished her work, SIMONE takes out a little package from her purse and begins nibbling on it. MME. LAURENCE speaks to SIMONE.)* Here, I'm going to give you a taste....

MIMI. Is this a day with or a day without, Madame Laurence?

MME. LAURENCE. Even when it's without I make it seem like it's with.

MIMI. How?

MME. LAURENCE. When I make a ragout, even if I don't have meat I put in a lot of sage so that later, when it comes back up, it comes back tasting like mutton.

MIMI. And when you fart?

MME. LAURENCE. *(primly)* Please, we're eating....

(GISELE returns.)

GISELE. *(Sees MARIE'S empty stool.)* Where's she gone?

MME. LAURENCE. She's eating out.

GISELE. You see, some people never deny themselves anything....

MIMI. Gisele! *(She signals to GISELE to button her lip. GISELE shrugs, takes out her lunchbox and brings it to the PRESSER.)*

PRESSER. So now I've got to do *two* servings?

GISELE. *(She says nothing; she fills an empty glass at the faucet behind the pressing table and carries it to the table, declaring:)* We ought to pool our money and buy some lithine so we could have bubbly water whenever we wanted.

MIMI. Buy, buy if you've got dough to throw away....

GISELE. I'm not one for scrimping when it's a question of health.... *(They sit and eat. From the courtyard a man is heard*

singing "The White Roses". They listen while eating. GISELE
opens the window. SIMONE remains seated. MIMI and GISELE
look up. The song continues through the end of the scene.)

    MAN. *(Sings "The White Roses".)*
HE WAS JUST A CHILD,
A SIMPLE PARIS KID.
HIS MOTHER WAS ALL THAT HE HAD.
SHE WAS VERY POOR, SAD AND HAUNTED EYES,
KNOCKED ABOUT BY LIFE'S CRUEL TROUBLES.
SHE LOVED EVERY FLOWER, ROSES BEST OF ALL,
SO EVERY SUNDAY MORNING
HE BOUGHT A BOUQUET OF WHITE ROSES
INSTEAD OF CANDY OR A TOY.
FIRST HE SMILED THEN HE HUGGED HER TIGHT
AND HE SAID WITH HIS EYES BURNING BRIGHT:

TODAY IS SUNDAY MORNING
THESE ARE FOR YOU, MAMAN
HERE ARE SOME WHITE ROSES
FOR YOU LOVE THEM SO
AND WHEN I AM A MAN
I'LL BUY ALL THAT I CAN
HUNDREDS OF WHITE ROSES
ALL FOR MY DEAR MAMAN.

BUT WHEN SPRING HAD COME
CRUEL DESTINY
STRUCK DOWN THE BLOND WORKING GIRL
SHE WAS TAKEN ILL AND A DOCTOR CAME
SAID SHE COULDN'T STAY AT HOME.
BREATHLESSLY HE RAN TO HIS MOTHER'S ROOM

WITH THE FLOWERS CLUTCHED IN HIS HANDS
BUT A NURSE IN WHITE STOPPED HIM AND
  WHISPERED:
"MY CHILD, YOUR MOTHER IS NO MORE."
THEN THE BOY FELL DOWN BY THE BED
AND HE SHED NOT A TEAR AS HE SAID:

TODAY IS SUNDAY MORNING
THESE ARE FOR YOU, MAMAN
I BROUGHT YOU WHITE ROSES
FOR YOU LOVE THEM SO
NOW THAT YOU'VE GONE AWAY
TO THAT GARDEN ABOVE
ALL OF THESE WHITE ROSES
YOU'LL HAVE THEM WITH MY LOVE.

  MIMI. Shall we give him some buttons?

  MME. LAURENCE. No, no, the poor man....

  MIMI. We'll put in twenty sous and some buttons; that'll make more noise.... *(Some of the women put on their jackets or drop their work over their shoulders to protect themselves from the cold. SIMONE has stopped working. The others are relaxing; MIMI is smoking. They all suddenly discover — even the PRESSER — that SIMONE is gently weeping.)*

Scene 3

NATURAL SELECTION

The end of an afternoon in 1946. All the women workers are present, but the PRESSER'S table is vacant.)

SIMONE. Yesterday a guy followed me.

MIMI. No? With the face you make when you're out alone....

GISELE. Let her talk.

MIMI. I ran into you the other day and, my God, you scared me; an industrious mouse: one, two, one, two....

SIMONE. You're right. Yesterday I was coming from the Red Cross; I had to leave a photo with them....

MIMI. Of yourself?

SIMONE. No, of my husband. It annoyed me; I don't have many more because of leaving them.... Anyway ... as usual I run, I don't look in front of me, I stand in line, it's my turn — hop — I'm outside already and there I bump into this guy.

MARIE. What was he like?

SIMONE. Just a guy.... I excused myself, he excused himself, we stammered a bit and I guess I must have smiled at him automatically.

GISELE. Ah la la, never smile ... never ... you've got to insult them....

SIMONE. I smiled, that was it, I was stuck, I couldn't get out of it: bla bla bla and bla bla bla....

MARIE. What did he say to you?

SIMONE. How do I know, I wasn't listening....

MME. LAURENCE. Was he vulgar?

SIMONE. Not really. He talked to me about my eyes ... more nonsense like that.... In the end I didn't dare step out of the metro.

MARIE. Did it happen on the street or in the metro?

SIMONE. I had to take the metro to get home....

GISELE. He followed you into the metro?

MME. LAURENCE. Some people have nothing to do.

SIMONE. That's just what I said to him: Don't you have anything better to do?

GISELE. You talked to him? Ah la la never talk....

SIMONE. Finally I got frightened.... I didn't dare get off at my station....

MARIE. Was there a crowd in the metro?

SIMONE. Not many, luckily....

MIMI. And what could he have done to you? A baby in the back through your coat?

SIMONE. You're a good one.... I'd like to have seen what *you* would have done—

GISELE. Not a chance — she's the one who collars them on the train and they have to scramble to avoid becoming a father.

MARIE. You can meet nice guys, too. I told everybody that it was at a dance, but it wasn't really true.... I met my fiancé on the bus .... we took the same bus every day....

(to SIMONE) So what happened?

SIMONE. I told a policeman that there's this guy who....

MIMI. And after that it was the cop who scared the shit out of you, right?

MME. LAURENCE. They're not like that.

MIMI. Oh yeah, pardon me; with a cop I'd have the shakes, but not with some ordinary guy who talked to me about my eyes....

MME. LAURENCE. They're not like that; they serve the public....

MIMI. Sure, tell her that....

GISELE. It's like everything else ... some cops are good and some are bad....

MIMI. *(overlapping)* Yap, yap, yap.

MME. LAURENCE. *(agreeing with GISELE)* Exactly!

SIMONE. In '42 the local police were helpful for the most part. There was one who insisted on carrying my bundle as far as the commissariat.

GISELE. They arrested you?

SIMONE. It wasn't me they wanted, it was my husband. But since he wasn't there they took me instead, along with the kids, to the commissariat, in the basement of City Hall.... There, the commissioner — very kind also — looked at my papers and told me to go back home because they weren't arresting French citizens; they hadn't received orders for that....

MME. LAURENCE. Your husband wasn't French? *(SIMONE shakes her head "no".)*

MIMI. Whew, little chicken, you nearly got your tail-feathers singed.

SIMONE. So I grabbed up my little bundle, my two kids and — only my oldest didn't want to leave like that; he was upset: "Isn't there anyone to carry Mama's package?" He shouted: "They made us come for nothing." I yanked him by the arm, I thought surely I'd pull it off. We ran all the way home.... *(She laughs. Everyone laughs.)*

GISELE. *(wiping her eyes)* Poor darling....

SIMONE. When we got home, there was something which I couldn't find: a large pocket watch that my husband got from his father and which always sat on the buffet in the kitchen....

MIMI. The one with the hobnailed boots snitched it from you....

SIMONE. That astonished me because they semed to be the good kind, helpful and all.... Not like those who came afterwards and took away my husband; they kicked down the door.

MARIE. Why did they do that?

SIMONE. They knocked, we didn't open, so.... The manager said it was up to me to repair the door. I've already repaired it, but you can still see the traces. Apparently that upsets the other tenants.... It would be better if he'd repaint the walls; they're peeling everywhere.... *(silence)*

MARIE. And the guy?

SIMONE. What guy?

MARIE. The guy, what was he like?

SIMONE. *(evasive)* Just a guy....

MARIE. Young?

SIMONE. Average.

MME. LAURENCE. You should have told him you have

children, that you were in a hurry; there's always a way to show them....

SIMONE. That's exactly what I did. I told him that I had two big kids. He says: "I love kids."

GISELE. Shit!

MME. LAURENCE. Everything depends on the tone of voice.

SIMONE. What's that supposed to mean?

MME. LAURENCE. *(repeats)* Everything depends on the tone of voice. *(brief silence)*

SIMONE. I didn't do anything bad, you understand.

MIMI. Oh, let her talk, it's all piss.

MME. LAURENCE. It's odd; that never happened to me. *(MIMI starts to laugh.)* Laugh, go ahead and laugh. They sense right away who they're dealing with.

SIMONE. All I did was tell him he was wasting his time. What else could I do?

MME. LAURENCE. No one is accusing you.

SIMONE. She's finally beginning to get on my nerves....

GISELE. You must never answer them, you must insult them, I mean it .... *insult....* *(Silence. They work with a great energy now, hurrying to finish the pieces in order to leave. Night has fallen. After having finished, they put away their pieces, put away their things, then they change and leave.)*

(HELENE has come in, and has gone to work during the workers' departure. On the pressing table there is a pile of clothing, unironed. HELENE, once the last worker has gone, stops and begins to pace, visibly unhappy. LEON enters and glances at the pressing table.)

LEON. He didn't come in all day?

HELENE. Who? *(LEON indicates the pressing table. HE-LENE shrugs.)*

LEON. You should tell him to come at regular hours, whether it's in the morning, or in the afternoon.... So we can know when we can count on him....

HELENE. Tell him yourself. *(She sits down at her work table.)*

LEON. Why? Why me? *(silence)* What does that mean, "Tell him yourself"? *(silence)*

HELENE. *(continuing to work)* If you have things to tell him, *you* tell him, period, that's all.

LEON. He doesn't iron well, he works badly, I shouldn't have hired him? *(silence)*

HELENE. *(with difficulty)* I can't look at him.

LEON. Don't look at him ... tell him without looking at him.... *(pause)* All right.... All right, I'll tell him, I'll tell him. *(He starts out but turns back and continues.)* "I can't look at him." What does that mean? He's a man like any other, yes or no? *(HELENE doesn't answer.)* What's the matter with him? What's the matter with him? He's as strong as a Turk; all day long he has a five-kilo iron in his hands, when he's not ironing here, he works the small press at Weill's and I'm sure that he has a third place for the early evening and a fourth for the night.... The only thing is: I want him to tell me when he'll be at Weill's and when he'll be here, that's all ... that's all. I wish I had nothing but workers like him, that's what I wish; of iron, he's of iron, never a word, never a complaint. He knows what it is to work, don't kid yourself, they know — those who've survived the camps. They know — that's called natural selection, madame. *(HELENE says nothing, she has stopped working; she goes out abruptly, wiping her eyes. LEON begins to follow her, then stops.)* That's what you get for trying to hold a serious discussion with her. *(He goes out, extinguishing the lights.)*

Scene 4

THE PARTY

In 1947. Late afternoon; everybody is at work. MARIE and GISELE, after having looked at the time, get up and prepare for the party.

GISELE. *(to those who are still working)* All right, all right, we're going to stop. *(then pushing the table against the wall)* Clear the way, we've got to set up.

MIMI. Is it all right if I finish my piece?

SIMONE. *(getting up)* You'll finish it tomorrow.

MIMI. *(continuing to work furiously)* Get her! She talks to men on the bus, but it's O.K. for me to lose a piece!

MARIE. *(laughing and snatching the work from MIMI'S hands)* Come on, stop!

MIMI. You really piss me off; am I the one who's getting married? *(During this time, MME. LAURENCE has gotten up, taken off her smock and slipped on her coat. The women continue preparing for the party. The PRESSER sets up a record player.)*

MARIE. *(fixing her make-up)* What are you doing, Madame Laurence?

MME. LAURENCE. I'm going home, dear.

MARIE. You're not staying for—

MME. LAURENCE. Unfortunately I can't choose the people I work with, but when it's a question of pleasure ... I value—

MIMI. When it comes to pleasure, she doesn't get to choose very often.

GISELE. *(combing her hair)* Come on, Madame Laurence, everybody here likes you a lot.

MME. LAURENCE. La, la, la, I know what I know.

MARIE. For my sake; it would please me very much.

MME. LAURENCE. I wish you happiness, my dear, and all that goes with it, but I've finished my day and I've a train to catch.

MIMI. *(tidying up)* Let her go then, if madame is too proud to have a drink with us.

SIMONE. *(after having fixed her make-up)* Madame Laurence, why not take advantage of occasions like this to make peace?....

GISELE. It's certainly not a day to make trouble!

MME. LAURENCE. As long as there are those who talk behind my back! *(She hesitates near the door.)*

GISELE, SIMONE & MARIE. Can you believe it! Go on then! She's imagining things, it's awful.

MIMI. *(to MME. LAURENCE)* Was that aimed at me?

SIMONE. Forget it, she wasn't talking about you!

MIMI. Was that aimed at me?

MME. LAURENCE. If the shoe fits....

MIMI. Believe me, sweetie, it's out of politeness that I talk behind your back.

MME. LAURENCE. Well, *you'd* better believe that I don't like it, and since we didn't raise pigs together, I'll ask you not to be so familiar.

MIMI. *(cutting her off)* What *you've* raised or not—

GISELE. C'mon, c'mon, shake hands and let's not talk about it anymore.

MIMI. Me, shake her hand! I should say not. I don't pretend to be something I'm not.

MME. LAURENCE. Everybody knows what you are.

MIMI. Good, there it is, that's it! You want to know face-to-face what I think of you behind your back?

MME. LAURENCE. I don't give a damn, believe me. Good night.

MIMI. *(preventing her from leaving)* Oh no, oh no! That would be too easy. She sows her shit, she fucks up our party and she expects to leave with her nose in the air? *(She pushes her back to the center of the workroom.)*

MME. LAURENCE. *(recoiling, hysterical)* Don't touch me!

SIMONE. Mimi! Madame Laurence!

MIMI. You want to know what we think? We're fed up with your airs, we're fed up, understand? And something else you'd better get through your thick skull is that you weren't born with that stool up your ass!

MME. LAURENCE. But what's she saying, what's she saying? Let me go....

MIMI. *(pursuing)* While we wreck our eyes all year under a light bulb, madame is next to the window by divine right! No more....

MME. LAURENCE. It's my place. I've no reason to change it. I won't change it.

MIMI. Tomorrow, it's my little cheeks that will be plopping there. Me, too, I've the right to make eyes at the concierge from time to time, don't I?

MME. LAURENCE. What?

(LEON enters, distracted. HELENE follows him; she is dressed up and made up.)

LEON. Now what's going on?

MME. LAURENCE. Monsieur Leon, Monsieur Leon, there it is, it's beginning again.

LEON. What's beginning again?

MME. LAURENCE. *(pointing at MIMI)* She wants to take my place.

MIMI. Why is she stuck to the window; why don't we take turns?

GISELE. One week one, one week another; that's the usual way, isn't it?

MME. LAURENCE. You see, you see, they're all starting.

LEON. What does it matter — near the window or not near the window, there's a good breeze, right?

MIMI. Exactly, we're afraid she'll get sick.

GISELE. We'd like to be able to breathe too.

MIMI. Monsieur Leon, it's impossible to see anything in your dump of a workroom. We're ruining our eyes, do you know what that's like? And Madame wants to monopolize the window and the sunlight.

LEON. But who's talking about sunlight; there's never any sun. In five minutes it will probably rain....

MIMI. To get the window open you have to beg her; Madame is cold. And when you want to close it, Madame is having her period, she feels faint ... shit!

GISELE. And then she takes advantage of it to look outside but she never wants to tell us what she sees. There,

I've said it and I'm sorry but....

LEON. *(opening the window and looking out)* But there's nothing to see, it's the courtyard, just the courtyard; there's absolutely nothing out there!

MIMI. Exactly; we want to see it ourselves.

LEON. Good, good... that's fine, that's fine, I get it; they tell me it's a party, they want me to stop early because Marie is getting married. I say yes, why not! I'm not an animal, I'm civilized. In short, it's the revolution. All right then, if that's the way it is, no more party, everybody sit down, back to work!

MIMI. *(Cuts him off, shouting.)* We want another light fixture; we don't want to ruin our eyes anymore or have any more favoritism here.... Got that? Good!... And we don't want your rotten stools anymore; we want some chairs, do you hear?

MME. LAURENCE. *(in a low voice)* Monsieur Leon, they have it in for me because my husband is a civil servant. That's the truth, go ahead and admit it; you're jealous!

SIMONE. But Madame Laurence, no one said anything about your husband.

MME. LAURENCE. Yes, my husband is a civil servant and I'm proud of it!

MIMI. *(Sings.)*

FROM VICHY COMES THE CALL: COLLABORATORS, ONE AND ALL.

MME. LAURENCE. *(Advances toward her, fists clenched.)* All right, then, all right then! *(Brief silence. MIMI turns her back.)*

LEON. Good, are you finished now, are you finished?

MIMI. *(to GISELE)* Now it's out in the open.

MME. LAURENCE. You've said plenty of other things which you wouldn't dare repeat.

MIMI. Oh yeah?

LEON. That's enough, now; that's enough!

MARIE. *(on the verge of tears)* You're wicked. The one time when I'm getting married.

LEON. Well done. That'll teach you to give yourself airs and make a fuss.... The result is that we've lost an hour and someone's crying.... *(MME. LAURENCE is taken aside by HELENE and SIMONE.)*

HELENE. Stay; make the little one happy.

MME. LAURENCE. No, no, no! They can insult me.... *(She makes a gesture of indifference.)* But when they insult my husband, never!

SIMONE. No one said anything about your husband, Madame Laurence; we've never even seen the man.

MME. LAURENCE. That's the last straw. *(in a low voice to both of them)* He saved some Jews, you know.

HELENE. Of course, of course.

MME. LAURENCE. And he didn't do it for money like some. Oh no.

SIMONE. Go on, take off your coat; you'll be cold when you go out.

MME. LAURENCE. *(Lets them take off her coat and continues in a lowered voice.)* He even went to warn them in advance.

HELENE. But who thinks about that anymore, Madame Laurence? Who still thinks about all that?

MME. LAURENCE. He took risks, he—

LEON. Helene, what about the machine operators, what are they doing?

MIMI. Ah, not the guys; guys aren't allowed in here.

LEON. What about *me* then?

MIMI. You're not a man; you're a monkey. Does Chee-chee want a banana?

LEON. *(like a monkey)* Ah! Ah! Ah! And the presser— I suppose he's not a man either! *(The PRESSER excuses his presence with a geature.)*

MIMI. In a harem, there always has to be a eunuch.

(The sewing machine OPERATORS enter.)

OPERATORS. So *here's* where we get drunk! Who's pouring?

LEON. Marie's the one getting married. So....

HELENE. The pressing machine girl has gone; we forgot to tell her....

OPERATORS. *(gathering around MARIE)* We're about to lose the only kissable one.... Where's your lover-boy, Marie, huh? *(While GISELE and MARIE get the bottles, SI-MONE goes to find the gift.)*

SIMONE. *(Waits for a silence, then:)* On behalf of all my friends....

MARIE. *(Bursts into tears and hugs SIMONE.)* You shouldn't have, you shouldn't have.

SIMONE. *(crying and hugging MARIE very tightly, all the while repeating)* Be happy, be happy....

MIMI. There it goes, they're off like waterfalls. Music, shit, music. *(She sings. They all embrace MARIE who cries looking at her unwrapped package.)*

MME. LAURENCE. *(in her coat and dry-eyed)* I also contributed toward the gift for the little one. My best wishes.

MARIE. *(hugging her hard)* Thank you, thank you. *(LEON puts on a record; it's a tango in yiddish.)*

MIMI. What's that?

LEON. A tango. Don't you know the tango?

SIMONE. *(explaining to MARIE and GISELE)* No, it's not German; it's yiddish.

GISELE. What's this yiddish?

SIMONE. It's what the Jews speak.

GISELE. And you speak it?

SIMONE. Yes.

GISELE. Then you're a Jew?

SIMONE. Sure.

GISELE. Wow, am I stupid. It's funny.

SIMONE. What's funny about it?

GISELE. Nothing. I knew that Monsieur Leon was; his wife too. But you.... I just can't grasp it.... It's.... It's strange, isn't it? But it's true? You are?... Then you could probably tell me what *really* went on between you and the Germans during the war? *(SIMONE remains silent.)* I mean ... how do you explain that you, the Jews, and they, the Germans.... At any rate, I don't know how to say it, but you had many ... many things in common, right? I was talking about it with my brother-in-law the other day, and he said to me: "Before the war, Jews and Germans were cut out of the same cloth." *(SIMONE doesn't answer; she looks at GISELE.)*

LEON. *(While dancing with MARIE, pushes the PRESSER toward SIMONE.)* You know how to dance?

PRESSER. Me?

LEON. *(pushing him into SIMONE'S arms)* Then ask her, ask her; she has only two children and she has a three-room apartment. *(The two couples begin to dance, but the music ends in their first step. LEON hurries to turn the record over.)*

HELENE. *(near the machine)* Don't you have anything else?

LEON. What?

HELENE. I don't know. Something more normal.

LEON. I don't know what you're trying to say.

HELENE. It's too yiddish.

LEON. What? *(HELENE shrugs her shoulders. He tries to control himself.)* What's too yiddish? *(HELENE shrugs her shoulders and then moves away. LEON follows her while the other song begins. It's a yiddish waltz.)* What's too yiddish?

HELENE. I didn't say anything, I didn't say anything. That sounds fine, that one!

LEON. Yes you did! Yes you did!

GISELE. *(Hugs MARIE.)* I've got to go home. It'll soon be your turn; ten minutes late and there's a crisis.

MME. LAURENCE. *(Gets up; she's a little tipsy.)* I'm going down with you. *(to MARIA)* You've got to train him, little one; you've got to train him, otherwise....

SIMONE. *(to the PRESSER)* Want to?

PRESSER. Can you dance to that?

SIMONE. It's a waltz.

PRESSER. I don't know if....

SIMONE. You have to turn, that's all.

PRESSER. You like that?

SIMONE. To dance?

PRESSER. No, yiddish? *(Clasps SIMONE.)* Shall we take the plunge?

SIMONE. Let's plunge. *(The PRESSER and SIMONE dance. LEON and HELENE, in a corner, are arguing.)*

Scene 5

NIGHT

*In 1947. The workroom is plunged into half-darkness. SIMONE
works in silence. Before her, some candles or a gasoline lamp.
The PRESSER sits by his pressing table and waits without
doing anything.*

SIMONE. I've enough more for quite a while.

PRESSER. *(grumbles)* No one is waiting for me.... *(silence)*

SIMONE. They still won't give me the death certificate; a
woman told me she was told that a missing-person certificate was enough.... But that depends ... to get a pension
it's not enough.... They always make us fill out new papers; you never know what your rights are.... No one
knows anything.... They toss us from one office to another. *(pause)* Because you've stood in line everywhere,
you end up knowing each other ... ah the tall stories go on
and on.... There are some who always know everything....
The mothers are the worst.... Did you have to go through
the Hotel Lutetia? *(He nods "yes".)* They sent me there at
the very beginning to get information; someone who
might have seen him, who — you know what I mean. The

photos, the — good. I was only there once, I didn't dare go back. There was a woman who grabbed me by the arm and shoved a photo in my face; the kind they take on Awards Day. I can still see the little boy — he was the same age as my eldest — in short pants, wearing a tie, clutching the book he was given as the prize for excellence." She was screaming: "He always got the prize for excellence." She didn't want to let go of me; she kept repeating: "Why are you crying? Why are you crying? Look, look, they're coming back — they'll *all* come back. It's God's will. It's God's will." Then another woman shouted at her and began to push her.... Someone ought to tell them there's no hope for the children. Yet there they are, they keep coming, they keep talking.... I've seen her time and again in the offices, more and more crazy.... I spotted another one of them — this one never likes to stand in line; she always wants to be waited on first. Once I said to her: "You know, Madame, we're all in the same boat here; no need to elbow your way to the front. There's enough unhappiness for everyone..." At the Prefecture, I met a Madame Levit, Levit with a "t" on the end. She was very nice, a good woman, but she was truly unlucky. Her husband was taken in '43, also, but he wasn't even Jewish, you see; hs name was Levit, that's all.... She hasn't stopped running since. At first during the war it was to prove that he was— *(She searches for the exact word.)*

PRESSER. *(whispers)* Innocent?

SIMONE. *(Nods "yes".)* And now, like us, she runs around just trying to find out what's become of him ... trying to get a little something.... She's a woman alone, with three children; she has no trade, she doesn't know how to do anything.... *(Silence. The PRESSER looks at her without saying anything. Silence.)* The hardest thing is not knowing ... thinking that perhaps he's lost somewhere, no longer able to remember even his name ... having forgotten me and the children. It happens ... it happens, but I tell myself that kid of illness cures itself with time.... The other day I was coming out of the market and I saw a man, with his back to me, holding a basket. I don't know why but I said to myself, just for a second, I thought: It's him! With a basket! It's funny because he wouldn't even go out to buy bread; he never ran errands. He didn't like to.... Anyway ... I mean you think of the times.... Here, I'm finished.... *(She hands him the piece. The PRESSER lights his lamp on the table and begins to iron it.)* Anyway, if the Prefecture doesn't want to give out the death certificate it means they still have some hope; it means even they aren't sure of anything. Otherwise they'd be only too happy to make out all the papers and file all the records, so that everyone would be in order and no one would have to mention it anymore. *(The PRESSER pounds on the back of the jacket to put it into shape and to force the steam out of it. He seems to strike some blows furiously, but in fact he's only doing what's necessary.)*

(LEON enters; he is joyous and excited.)

LEON. So you're fighting it out in the dark, huh? Our President fires some cabinet members, there's a strike and — hop! — all France finds itself in blackness; happily they've left us the gas....

PRESSER. *(Hands the jacket to LEON.)* There it is....

LEON. *(Forming a coat-hanger with his open hands, delicately receives the jacket under the shoulders, then bringing it closer to the light, he turns it around.)* A new model again: pockets on the backs of the sleeves... oh, well, if that pleases them and if it brings in orders, who am I.... *(as he exits)* I'll be a minute; just the time it takes to dispose of the self-styled new model with the self-styled representative. I don't like him at all; he's a .... *(He makes the gesture of tightening a necktie. SIMONE hasn't budged; she remains seated, eyes fixed.)*

PRESSER. *(Sits down next to her. Silence. He speaks with difficulty.)* He left when?

SIMONE. '43

PRESSER. End of '43?

SIMONE. *(Shakes her head "no".)* On the missing-person certificate it says: "Left Drancy in March, 1943...." *(a pause)*

PRESSER. They say for where?

SIMONE. In the direction of Lublin Maidanek... *(silence)*

PRESSER. How old was he?

SIMONE. Thirty-eight. We married late; we were ten years apart.

PRESSER. Did he look older or younger? *(She doesn't understand.)* Than his age?

SIMONE. *(without looking at him)* Perhaps a little more when they took him; he was a convalescent. He stayed at Compiegne for a little while as a prisoner of war. He got sick over there. Then they released him. When he got back to Paris, he got some papers for himself at the Jewish Association so he'd be legal. It's funny: he who'd lived in France for years without identity papers, decides he wants to be absolutely legal. At the Association they gave him a sort of residence permit. He wasn't French; he was still Rumanian, so in the end they wrote: "Country of Origin: Rumania".

PRESSER. *(without looking at her)* He wear glasses?

SIMONE. Yes, but not all the time.

PRESSER. His hair? *(She doesn't understand.)* Did he have all his hair?

SIMONE. A little bald perhaps, but he looked good that way. *(silence)*

PRESSER. Face the fact that he never got beyond the camp gate. *(brief pause)* When we arrived, those who survived the trip were separated into two groups .... those who were going to enter the camp and the others. We, we left on foot. The others, the majority, climbed into trucks. At the time we envied them.... *(He stops.)* The trucks took them directly to the showers.... They didn't have time to realize.... *(a pause)* They've told you about the showers? *(silence)*

SIMONE. How can you be sure? *(The PRESSER is silent.)* Everyone says some of them are still going to come back. There are some everywhere: in Austria, in Poland, in Russia, and they're being taken care of. they're being rehabilitated before being sent home! *(The PRESSER shakes his head in silence.)* Thirty-eight is not old, not old at all. Granted, they did what you said to the old, to those who couldn't work anymore, to the women, to the children ... everyone knows all that, but—

(She is interrrupted by LEON, who enters carrying a tray on which there's tea, a liter of eau-de-vie and some dry cakes. SI-MONE rises, slips her coat over her smock, and goes out after

*having placed her hand, in passing, on the PRESSER'S
shoulder. The PRESSER hasn't moved.)*

LEON. *(flabbergasted)* She's stubborn that one! *(He goes
out after shouting.)* How about a drink? Wait, don't go home
all alone. At least let someone go with you. *(He returns.)*
She's gone. She's nuts, right? What's the matter with her?
If she didn't want to stay she should have said so.... There
it is: ask for extra work today ... if you've agreed to do it, do
it willingly, right? I would have done it myself, this miserable piece. You saw that.... *(toward the door)* Go on, smart-
ass. *(to PRESSER)* Did she say something to you?

PRESSER. It was me who talked to her.

LEON. Ah! Good! Ah, good.... You want some tea or a
glass of.... *(He shows him the liquor bottle.)*

PRESSER. *(without getting up)* I'm going home, too....

LEON. *(serving him)* No, no I absolutely insist. How
about a glass of ... huh? *(The PRESSER doesn't move. LEON
serves himself.)* You did well, you did well.... Me, too, I've
wanted to speak to her for a long time, but....

PRESSER. *(as if to himself)* If only you could cut out
your tongue.

LEON. Yes, you're right: "If only you could cut out your
tongue." *(He shouts suddenly as if he's suffocating.)* Helene!
Helene! *(to the PRESSER)* What do you want? In this
world, a person needs a certain amount of give.... *(Points to
SIMONE'S stool.)* That's what she's missing ... so inevitably
she.... *(He searches for words.)* She....

PRESSER. *(rising)* I'm going home....

LEON. Out of the question; we're going to drink together. Otherwise.... *(He makes a vague gesture. He turns over
two glasses.)*

(HELENE enters wearing no make-up; she has a bathrobe over her nightgown.)

HELENE. Has Simone left?

LEON. Yes. *(pointing to the PRESSER, in a low voice)* He spoke to her. *(HELENE looks at the PRESSER without saying anything. LEON raises his glass and offers the other to the PRESSER, who accepts it mechanically.)* Go on, drink, drink. *(They drink.)* I wanted to speak to her myself, yes ... yes, only.... I was afraid of what I might say — really afraid! I plan to say something kind, full of good sense and human understanding, but what comes out is a disgusting mess. It's as if I had verbal diarrhea. It's horrible; it always happens like that. *(He spits, then to HELENE.)* Isn't that ture? Oh, I know myself, believe me, I know myself....

HELENE. Please stop drinking. Do you want—

LEON. *(indignant)* Me? I haven't drunk anything.... *(He turns toward SIMONE'S stool and howls suddenly.)* On the shelves where the German housewives keep their stock of brown soap, there's where he is, that's where you have to look for him; not in offices, not in files, not on lists....

HELENE. *(Rises and pushes him with all her strength to get him to sit down again.)* That's enough; have you gone crazy or what? The PRESSER hasn't reacted.)

LEON. *(Tries to laugh, wagging his finger at her.)* Tss tss tss ... she's never had the slightest sense of humor. Never ... what can you do: a German Jew? Each country gets the yids it deserves. *(He laughs.)* The dregs of the dregs of the earth, madame, that's what you are. *(He pretends to spit on her.)*

HELENE. *(Shrugs and murmers.)* Polack humor! Very

subtle.... *(She yawns.)*

PRESSER. I can't stay in bed in the morning....

LEON. Why? It'll be a strike for Weill, too, you know!

PRESSER. I got into the habit; I can no longer manage to stay in bed in the morning.... *(Silence. The PRESSER pours himself a glass.)*

LEON. *(getting a drink)* That's it, that's it, let's drink, let's drink. *(He sings quietly.)*

LET'S DRINK A GLASS, LET'S DRINK IT, TWO JOLLY COMPANIONS OF BURGUNDY. *(He sighs and then picks up his drinking song.)*

HELENE. *(without stirring)* Good, as for me, I'm going to bed. *(She remains seated. She yawns.)*

LEON. That's right, that's right, run to the free zone, go, go. That one went to rejoin her mother with the peasants. Me, I didn't want to go; no, I stayed ... the whole war in Paris, me, monsieur! I even had false papers and everything; Richard, I was called, Leon Richard ... yes.... I went everywhere; some days I was myself wearing my Jewish star; some days I was Richard without the star. I even worked a little under that name at a fashionable dress shop.... An Italian.... People said to me: "Be careful, Monsieur Leon," but I said to myself, even if I'm caught what could they do to me; another kick in the ass?.... No one realized at that time ... we were blind ... totally blind.... I even went to play cards in a cafe with some Armenians.... And then at the end of '43, beginning of '44, people everywhere began to say that they were taking us away to burn us. That's when I began to get the shakes for real! They sealed off the free zone; our last escape was gone.... One day I come home and the concierge he signals to me

not to go up. They were up there; three youngsters with
berets. I saw them come back down, disappointed. They
said several words to the concierge. He's the one who hid
me in a room on the top floor; he brought me things to eat
and the news. I stayed there, blinds down, and waited like
a mole, and waited.... And then one day, knock, knock,
knock. Who's there? "Monsieur Leon, this is it — it's all
over; the Krauts are busy making themselves scarce." It
hit me like a bombshell. *(a pause)* I raced into the street
like a real madman — you realize I had nowhere to go— I
looked at the people, at the faces above all; they seemed
happy, certainly but, how can I say it? *(a pause)* There was
still gunfire here and there, especially from the roofs. I
went from one barricade to another ... one time they even
stuck a rifle in my hands, they soon took it away from me
because — according to them — I was holding it upside
down.... And then somehow I fell in with a group near a
truck. A very young man was climbing into it, arms high
in the air, hands on his head. It was a blond German
youngster. We exchanged glances and I don't know why
but I had the impression that this asshole was asking me
for help. The French soldiers who were making him get
into the truck shoved him a little to give themselves a
more military air. The women were making jokes and he
seemed to shout at me: "And you, yes, you who know,
you who have some experience, help me, teach me." Suddenly I threw myself toward him, screaming, "Ich bin
yude, ich bin yude, bin leibedick!" Then he closed his
eyes and turned his head away and disappeared in the
back of the truck.... Suddenly panic broke out; the women
dragged their brats into the shelter of the doorways:

"Another German, a civilian and a surly one at that!" The soldiers surrounded me; the leader, pointing his machine-gun at my chest, repeated: papers, papers.... I tried to laugh; a miserable rumble came from my belly, and after I caught my breath, I said as calmly as possible: "I am a Jew, monsieur officer of the resistance. I wanted him to know that I was Jewish and alive. That's all, that's why I shouted ... excuse me...." The leader looked at me for a minute without moving. I saw clearly in his eyes that he didn't understand why I'd shouted, that undoubtedly he would *never* understand. I was afraid that he'd ask me to explain; I stepped backward. Finally he gave the signal and the soldiers jumped into the truck, magnificent!... I could still feel the others staring; I spread my arms, lowered my head and then, despite myself, my body — my whole body — apologized. A lot of good it did me to repeat to myself that it was over, that I was again a free man with nothing to do.... Then a voice, very much "old soldier" from Verdun, said very loudly, detaching each syllable: "Here in France, we respect prisoners of war!" My belly rumble became more resounding. Then I became transparent — you know, like the invisible man in the movie, and I left them all together: all those people who respect prisoners of war, the Geneva Convention, the Hague meetings, the Munich agreements, the German-Soviet pacts, and the cross, *all* the crosses, and I went home. A few days later the German *(He indicates HELENE with his chin.)* returned and we laid out our first inter-facing in a kind of felt, half-cardboard, half-blotting paper; at the moment they weren't difficult to do because everything pulled apart like little loaves of bread. It was a good

time except that you found neither fabric nor supplies....
(silence) And you, how did they take you?

PRESSER. *(after a time)* They took me!

LEON. *(Nods agreement. Silence.)* In the beginning I did it
all, with Helene. I was the cutter, the presser, the machine
operator, and Helene worked by hand. After that we took
on the cop's wife.... *(He points to MME. LAURENCE'S place.)*
After that we stumbled onto the crazy one.... *(He points out
MIMI'S place.)* Later, there was an operator who brought
me his cousin, and then, and then, voila, from thread to
needle as they say, I found myself in shit up to here.
(silence)

PRESSER. *(getting up)* I'm going home. *(He takes a step.)* I
won't be coming in Monday.

LEON. Good, what do you want me to say to you? You
want your Monday, *take* your Monday; take advantage of
me like the others.... What do you want me to do
about it?

PRESSER. *(Takes another step.)* You'll have to look for
another presser! *(He gathers up his things and prepares to
leave.)*

LEON. What, what does that mean? What does that
mean? Are you looking for a raise? Speak frankly with me,
okay; none of that between us, not between us! *(He is on the
verge of tears and holds the PRESSER by the arm.)*

PRESSER. I'll come by during the week to settle up; get
my tally-sheet ready.

LEON. But you're crazy, what's gone wrong? Are you
mad at someone? Is it me? Have I said something? Somebody's gotten on your nerves?

PRESSER. No, no, it's.... *(He doesn't finish his phrase and makes no gesture.)*

LEON. At least finish out your week, we'll see after that. We're not savages, right? We'll talk about it again.... Things are going to work out.... Just give me a chance to catch my breath, all right?

PRESSER. *No ... no ... it's better like this....Salut, Leon.*

LEON. *(without shaking his hand)* You're not comfortable here, you're not comfortable?

PRESSER. Yes, yes, very comfortable ... doesn't matter, Salut. *(He leaves.)*

LEON. *(following him)* They warned me, they told me never to get involved with your kind. Never! You're all crazy, all crazy. But you're not the only one who has suffered; shit, not the only one! There's *me* too; I've done dirty things in order to survive.... *(He comes back and knocks over the bottle and teapot; he howls, kicking them.)* Ah shit!!

INTERMISSION

Scene 6

THE COMPETITION

The workroom. A day in 1948, before noon. The pressing table is unoccupied. GISELE stands working at the pattern table. MARIE is very obviously pregnant.

GISELE. *(while working)* I said to her: "You can do what you want later on, when you're married; right now *I'm* still giving the orders...."

MARIE. What did she answer?

GISELE. *(shrugging her shoulders)* Nothing. She was already on the landing; I don't even know if she heard me.

MIMI. That's what you get when you bawl them out all the time.

GISELE. Sure, it's easy for *you* to talk!

MARIE. You know, it's normal at her age to want to go out ... when you're married you can't go out as much....

MME. LAURENCE. You'd like to "go out" in your condition?

MARIE. I didn't say that....

GISELE. "At her age"; you'd better believe that at her

age I couldn't stay out late.

MIMI. And look where it got you! *(GISELE looks at her without understanding.)* Would you like your daughter to turn out like you?

GISELE. I'm not so bad; there are worse. I've got no complaints....

MME. LAURENCE. You don't look your age, that's certain....

GISELE. *(annoyed)* Thanks a lot. *(Silence. Then to herself)* Go out, go out, that's all they can say. Me, I'd rather go home....

MIMI. To fight with your Jules?

GISELE. We don't fight all the time!

MIMI. Oh, I can see that from here: a hot love affair! *(She hums a java.)*

SIMONE. *(to GISELE)* And your youngest?

GISELE. Oh, she's got no problems.

MIMI. She hasn't got the itch yet.

GISELE. *(to MIMI)* Oh, how disgusting you can be! It's easy to see you don't have any kids.... *(to SIMONE)* She's doing well in school and all in all, she's fine — knock on wood ... let's hope it lasts....

MARIE. What do you want your daughters to do later?

MIMI. *(in an undertone to SIMONE and MARIE)* There's always the sidewalk!

GISELE. You see, I'm not complaining but I wouldn't want them to end up like me, pulling a needle the whole blessed day. Pardon me for being blunt but it's not a very interesting life.... Frankly, I'd prefer that they learn to stitch by machine; you wear yourself out less, it pays better and the work is more interesting, right?

MME. LAURENCE. Machine operator? It's a man's job!

MIMI. Why, do you have to pump the pedal with your balls?

MME. LAURENCE. *(Lets out an "oh" of suffering while the others burst out laughing.)* It's a pleasure to have a serious discussion with you; you can see immediately what fascinates you....

MIMI. Balls? They don't fascinate me more than something else; actually somewhat less.... I thought I understood, that's all....

MME. LAURENCE. *(between her teeth)* Always dirty things....

MIMI. They're not dirty things, Madame Laurence; of course you have to run them under the water from time to time, otherwise — like everything else — they end up smelling.... You ought to tell your husband: when he washes his ass he ought to rinse his organ as well.... *(The others are now under the table, crying with laughter.)*

MME. LAURENCE. *(covering her ears)* Please don't talk to me anymore, don't talk to me anymore, leave me alone; I'm sorry I said whatever it was. Oh my God, my God! *(MME. LAURENCE drops her work and runs toward the door.)*

MIMI. What do you know: maybe she's going to get her pedal fixed....

(MME. LAURENCE goes out, bumping into LEON, who enters, a jacket under his arm.)

GISELE. *(who didn't hear MIMI'S last reply)* What did she say?... What did she say? (SIMONE and MARIE are still *crying with laughter, wiping their eyes, and gasping. MIMI works seriously. GISELE begs her to repeat her last line.*

LEON. *(Looks at SIMONE, MARIE and GISELE, who blow their noses, each one louder than the other. Then he asks:)* Are you laughing or crying?

MARIE. We don't know anymore, monsieur Leon; we don't know anymore. *(She groans.)*

GISELE. Something to drink, help!

MIMI. *(serious)* It's hard to keep them quiet; I do what I can, but there are some days.... *(gesture of futility)*

LEON. *(With an unaccustomed calm, he waits for MME. LAURENCE to come back to her seat and then he lets go.)* Good ... in your opinion, Madame, whom are we sewing for, the dead or the living? *(No response. LEON studies the jacket from every angle — it's a poor specimen.)* If we're sewing for the dead, I'd say that this garment is a very fine garment for a dead man.... but just between us, a dead man can do very well without garments, right? You toss him into a bit of rag, roll him up, and — plop! — into the hole. You can even save money on the rag and on the hole. We know about that, right? If we're sewing for the living, it's necessary to make provisions for certain gestures which a living man will inevitably have to make: like moving an arm, sitting down, breathing, rising, buttoning, unbuttoning. I won't even mention wartime when frequently the living, in order to remain living, are obliged to raise both arms in the air at the same time. No, I'm talking about ordinary moves, made during ordinary life, in ordinary clothes. Look at this piece; Monsieur Max has just returned it to me with a little paper pinned on the back. Gisele, will you please read what's on this paper. It's written in big letters. *(He shows her the paper.)*

GISELE. *(reads)* "This is sewing for the dead."

LEON. A customer had just left.... *(brief silence, then:)* That the lining of the sleeve, yes, Madame Simone, has split.... All right, I know it's not serious, not yet worth crying over; these things happen. That's what the salesman immediately said; a poor quality thread, a stitch too loose, let's go on.... Next the buttons fell off one-by-one when the customer wanted to.... *(He makes the gesture of buttoning.)* Automatically, the customer cast a glance down at the buttonholes. Yes, madame Mimi, look at them, as well; buttonholes done by hand?

MIMI. Sure; what's the matter with them?

LEON. You could say that they shit and vomit at the same time.... That's what's the matter. Next he raised his eyes and saw himself in the mirror. Then he tore this thing off his body, raced out of the store, and threw himself head-first into a store run by our competitor. Perhaps you've already heard of the competition; you know, all those people who are a lot less expensive because they have less overhead.... Seeing the customer leave on the run, the owner of the store dumped all the merchandise which he had just received right into Max's lap, with this little paper pinned to the back, and then he, too, went running to the competition for his order. Monsieur Max received the package, he examined it, he called me, I examined it next and I must admit that the client was right. It's sewing for the dead! *(Silence. He begins again, in a professional manner.)* Now I must warn you, those who wish to continue sewing for the dead are going to have to do it somewhere besides here.... From now on, my workroom will dedicate itself soley to the living; and those people, believe me, want something for their money today. The time is over when we stuck them with the worst rubbish: raincoats with two left sleeves, jackets which button in back, etc., etc. Fini! The war has been over a long time; with a little luck we'll get another one soon. Who knows; things are going beautifully everywhere.... We are no longer in the post-war era; we are once again in the pre-war period. Everything is normal again, everything is available today — at all prices. They're even talking about ending rationing. Now I demand a minimum of professional integrity, you understand ... a minimum. *(He puts on the jacket. It is too big for him and hangs badly on all sides.)* Look at this, look at this "half-size"! One shoulder's already on the second floor while the other's still in the basement.... Madame Laurence, it's necessary to pay a little attention to what you're doing when you work instead of constantly watching the others....

GISELE. The color looks good on you....

LEON. "Color?!" On top of everything else, you're making fun of me?

GISELE. No, no, I'm sincere, monsieur Leon. *(MARIE lets out a crazy nervous laugh.)*

LEON. *(howls)* It's over now, enough joking. Each piece will be checked, and re-checked and re-checked, and if the stitches are too large or if it's bungled you'll work on it again until it's right! Doing and undoing are both work but they're not paid the same; you're going to learn that right now. Oh you've had a cushy life so far but all that's finished, you understand, fini! I want it to be hard labor here from now on, like it is elsewhere — like everywhere

— like at our competitor's. I've been a sucker, right? *(SIMONE has risen as discreetly as possible, placed the piece she's just finished on the pressing table, taken off her smock, and slipped on her coat. LEON sees her near the door.)* What! Sit down! Sit down immediately. What's that? What's that mean? You come in, you go out; it's a revolving door here?

SIMONE. I've an errand to run and since it's almost lunchtime, I thought I'd take advantage of....

LEON. I'm the one who decides when it's lunchtime or not.

SIMONE. I warned madame Helene that I'd have to be gone; it's important.

LEON. I don't want to know about it. Around here I give the orders; I'm the one you've got to ask!

SIMONE. You weren't there so I asked your wife.

LEON. *(shouts)* You ask *me*, you ask *me*, and me — I say no, there! When someone spends half the time on errands or on sick leave—

SIMONE. *(protesting)* I had to stay away from work for eight days once in three years and even then I brought things home to finish.

LEON. Blah, blah, blah. If you can't stick to your job, we can't let you occupy a stool here. Positions like this are hard to come by; every day I get requests, there's work here all year — no off seasons. Either do the job or get out for good! If you want to groan, or cry, or run errands, this isn't the place. This isn't the Bureau for Widows and Dependent Children. I want you to work, to turn out impeccable merchandise which we can deliver and which won't be thrown back in our teeth.... Who's going to have to swallow this whole series Max got back? It's me, me! I don't want to hear laughter anymore, or shouts, or tears, or songs; from now on no one will be allowed to take off an hour, you hear me, an hour, even if your children perish, even if your old folks rot, even if your husbands blow up, I don't want to know about it, understand; for errands you have Saturday afternoon and Sunday.

SIMONE. *(Bursts out, on the verge of tears.)* The offices are closed!

MIMI. *(to SIMONE)* What are you arguing with him for, honey? Go on, don't be afraid; I'll tell you how it comes out. *(SIMONE glances at LEON and he turns away. SIMONE goes out. Silence. LEON sits down in SIMONE'S place and remains there for a moment without saying anything, as though empty. The workers return to their work again in silence.)*

LEON. *(to MIMI)* You've got a big mouth, eh?

MIMI. It's fine, thanks; I do what I can.... *(silence)*

LEON. Then explain to me with your big mouth what she's going to gain by ruining her health running like that from one office to another....

MIMI. She has a right to a pension, doesn't she? A woman alone with two children!

LEON. It's here, her pension is here! *(He taps on the table.)* She stays an extra hour every evening, she runs her errands every day and she gets her pension, right?

GISELE. She can't stay any later.

LEON. Why, who does that upset; we're open, I stay myself....

MIMI. Yes, but when you want to eat, all you have to do is slide your two flat feet under the table; your stew is hot, whereas she has to run errands and get supper for her kids.

LEON. Where there's a will, there's a way; you have to know where your interest lies. Why should they give her a pension, in whose honor?

GISELE. Her husband was deported, wasn't he?

LEON. But he wasn't even French, madame, not even French. She has a right to nothing! They provide pensions for the French, not for stateless persons of Rumanian origin; who's going to provide it, huh, who — the French? Why? The Rumanians? Don't know him, the Rumanians; he left Rumania when he was twelve. They don't give a damn, the Rumanians. The stateless? Ah, the stateless can't help; they all left with him, the stateless, and those who came back, they're all cracked like the former presser, you remember? Anyway, who still cares about all that? New camps are springing up, no one's got time to spend on the old ones when already there are new ones.

MIMI. She has been to a legal committee; they're going to tell her.

LEON. That's right, a legal committee ... they're going to tell her.... *(He makes a gesture which seems to say: "Who am I talking with?" He gets up, gathers up the jacket which was on the floor, hesitates, then wads it into a ball and throws it under the pressing table. The workers work without looking at him.)*

MIMI. *(Keeps her eyes on her work.)* It's not the sewing which is off; it's his cutting. He cuts any which way.... Are my buttonholes to blame if it hangs badly, if the sleeves are screwed up? Where are you going to find buttonholes like that?... If there was a competition I'm sure that I'd hold the world championship for buttonholes.... Look, look, I'm not shitting you: wouldn't you say it lives, that it sees you, that it lacks only speech, and at that, I don't even have cord — just rotten thread which breaks and knots.... Honestly ... there are days ... I ask myself *why* am I doing this? *(ironically)* Obviously because it's fashionable.... I upset myself and.... I've nothing.... I've nothing.... I don't have nylons.... I don't have a suit.... I don't have soap, nothing.... First of all, I want some chocolate. I want some chocolate!

GISELE. Hey, what's the matter with you, Mimi?

MARIE. Have *you* got a craving?

MIMI. What, what, aren't I right? The end of rationing? For *them* it is, but what do we have, what do we have; there isn't even toilet paper in the johns, not even toilet paper....

(HELENE enters with more jackets. MME. LAURENCE and GISELE try to warn MIMI by coughing.)

MIMI. *(After noticing HELENE'S presence, immediately curbs herself.)* What, what.... I'm not ashamed. I can say it before madame Helene: it's the cutting which is off, it's the cutting, not my buttonholes.... *(HELENE continues to hang jackets on the high bar, perhaps those which MAX has just returned.)*

Scene 7

THE DEATH CERTIFICATE

1949. Afternoon. Working are: MIMI, MME. LAURENCE, JEAN—the "new presser", and HELENE at her pattern table. SIMONE is in the midst of taking off her coat and slipping on her smock.

HELENE. You have it? *(SIMONE nods "yes".)* Let me see it. *(SIMONE takes a sheet of paper out of a large envelope which she hands carefully to HELENE. SIMONE sits down and begins to work. HELENE reads in a low voice.)* Death certificate ... by a judgment of the civil tribunal of the Seine ... on these grounds the tribunal states and affirms monsieur ... deceased at Drancy, Seine. Deceased at Drancy? Why have they put deceased at Drancy?

SIMONE. *(without looking up from her work)* That's how they do it!

HELENE. *(raising her voice in spite of herself)* What do you mean, that's how they do it? *(SIMONE doesn't answer; she stitches with great energy. HELENE reads on to the end.)* Deceased at Drancy, Seine, March 3, 1943. What does that mean? He slipped on a sidewalk in Drancy, Seine, and

67

died? *(JEAN approaches, takes the death certificate and reads it. HELENE tries to control herself. SIMONE works indifferently.)*

JEAN. *(after having read it)* They put down the last place where the deceased left a trace ... legal.... That's the date and the place of his departure for.... That's so it will be more.... *(searching for the words)* more ... legal.

HELENE. *(cutting him off)* The date of the departure for where? For where? They don't say that it's a date of departure.... They say deceased at Drancy, Seine, period, that's all. *(JEAN goes back to the pressing table without saying anything. Silence. HELENE now walks up and down the workroom and then returns to SIMONE.)* In your missing-persons certificate, it's clear he left Drancy the third of March '43 in the direction of Lublin-Maidanek, right? I didn't invent it. Why didn't they put that again? Simply that?

SIMONE. *(after a time)* On a death certificate you can't put in the direction of....

HELENE. Why?

SIMONE. It's necessary to be more precise.

HELENE. Why? *(SIMONE doesn't answer; she works more and more energetically. Silence. HELENE suddenly shouts.)* You've got to refuse! You must refuse, you don't have to accept that on top of everything, you don't have to accept that.

(LEON arrives, the cutting scissors in his hand.)

LEON. What's going on, what is it now? What's she done?

HELENE. *(holding out the certificate)* Here, read!

LEON. What's that?

HELENE. Read.

LEON. *(Skims the paper and returns it to HELENE.)* Very good ... very good.... With that she won't have to run from one office to another anymore; maybe she'll be able to stay put from time to time, right there *(He points to the stool.)*

HELENE. *(giving him back the paper)* Read to the end!

LEON. I've read, I've read to the end. It's good, very good, all the stamps are there, it's perfect!

HELENE. Nothing there shocks you?

LEON. Shocks me? You think it's the first time I've seen a death certificate? *(He laughs derisively and shakes his head.)* If I only had as many orders this winter as I've already seen dea—

HELENE. *(crying out)* Deceased at Drancy! Deceased at Drancy!

LEON. So? Drancy or somewhere else.... It's a paper, isn't it?

HELENE. Poor idiot; "Drancy or somewhere else." But if the truth doesn't exist on their papers with all their stamps and all their official signatures, look ... Tribunal of the Seine.... Clerk of the Court ... registered ... certified ... then no one got sent over there, no one ever got into their railroad cars, no one was burned; if they're simply deceased at Drancy, or Compiegne, or at Pithiviers; who will remember them?! Who will remember them?!

LEON. *(in a low voice)* They will be remembered, they will be remembered. There's no need for papers, and above all there's no need to shout.

HELENE. Why do they lie, why? Why not simply put the truth; why not put "thrown alive into the flames?" Why?...

LEON. A paper, it's a paper; she needs this paper in order to try to get a pension, that's all. Maybe she's got no right to this pension, certainly no right, but she wants to try, she still wants to run and run again to the offices; it's stronger than she is, she loves it — to fill up files, card-indexes, papers, it's her personal vice and that paper is good for nothing else ... for nothing else ... it's a paper for obtaining other papers, that's all!

HELENE. And her children, how will they know? They'll see "deceased at Drancy", and that's all?

LEON. They'll know, they'll know; they always know too much.

HELENE. Certainly with you, the less one knows the better one gets along.

LEON. Those who ought to know, will never know; and we, we already know too much — much too much....

HELENE. Who ought to know according to you?

LEON. *(after a pause, in an undertone)* The others.

HELENE. Which others?

LEON. Don't scream like that, this is a workroom here; we're here to work, to work, not to philosophize.... *(to SIMONE)* And you, settle down ... why do you have to go spreading out your papers here; we don't give out pensions here; we work here, period, that's all ... no need for certificates or documents.

HELENE. Stop shouting at her; I'm the one who asked her for it.

LEON. And who are you: judge, witness, lawyer, Minister for the Veterans and War Victims? You want to set everything to rights. You, with your big mouth, huh? Straighten out *my* problems first, then if you've got a little time left, you can worry about *their* problems.

HELENE. What problems do you have?

LEON. Me? None! I'm happy, so happy I'm dying from so much happiness. What problems do I have, what problems do I have?... And who's going to remember me, madame, huh, who's going to remember me, in your opinion, who? *(HELENE goes out. LEON sighs and then moves restlessly around the workroom; everyone works in silence. LEON questions SIMONE.)* Everything all right?

SIMONE. *(Shrugs her shoulders as if all that didn't concern her at all.)* Fine....

LEON. Good ... good. *(He exits.)*

Scene 8

THE MEETING

In 1950. The workroom working at top speed.

LEON. *(to JEAN while unhooking some jackets hung at the back of the room above the pressing table)* Can you stay later tonight?

JEAN. I'm leaving at 6:30....

LEON. Six-thirty; you're a civil servant now?

JEAN. Is today Friday?

LEON. That's right, it's Friday, the day before Saturday.

JEAN. I leave at 6:30 every Friday. I have a meeting.

LEON. You have a meeting Friday night and I've got to deliver Saturday morning! *(JEAN doesn't rise to this; he works calmly. LEON shrugs his shoulders and then reaches the door. On the verge of going out, he changes his mind and then the idea connects.)* Your revolution, you're going to start it tonight, at this meeting?

JEAN. I don't think so.

LEON. *(a sigh)* Too bad! It would be a good excuse for delivering late tomorrow morning.... A pity.... It's just a meeting to discuss then, to prepare? For once couldn't they discuss a little bit without you?

JEAN. No!

LEON. You're such a big leader, that even to discuss they can't do it without you?

JEAN. *(slamming down the iron)* If you want a presser who works day and night to please you....

LEON. No one works here to please me....

JEAN. We're not married, eh! It's not as if jobs were scarce....

LEON. *(using the workers as witness)* It's a real disease: all the pressers want to leave here! This table is no good, it leans; the iron is too heavy, you want tea at five o'clock; this monkey isn't pleasant enough! *(He makes a horrible grimace; the workers protest and offer him bananas.)*

JEAN. Friday, every Friday I have a meeting and I go at 6:30.

LEON. Go, go ahead leave, leave; may God protect you! You know what, we're going to reassign the tasks: You, you go to your meeting and concern yourself with the happiness of all humanity and me, I'll come back here tonight and concern myself with tomorrow's delivery. There, how about that? At least don't forget to tell them that regularly, every year, I buy an ad in the Peasant Workers' Almanac and I support the Labor Festival which I never attend, however, because it never fails to rain.

JEAN. Don't worry — I'll fix it so they shoot you among the last!

LEON. My wife, too?

JEAN. Your wife, too.

LEON. Thanks, it's good to feel you're protected.

Simone, you stay with me to sew on buttons; at least you don't have a meeting. *(He goes out without waiting for an answer.)*

MIMI. You're stupid — why do you take that? Why don't you tell him to go to hell?

GISELE. Can't he ask his wife?

MIMI. Think — she might chip her nail polish. *(SI-MONE stitches, indifferent.)*

GISELE. And your kids?

SIMONE. When they don't see me Friday evenings, they come looking for me.

MIMI. Fine; everything's perfect, if you like that....

JEAN. You could shit on her head, ahe'd still say thanks.... You have rights you haven't even found out about; how are you going to make them respect you? *(Silence. Everyone works. Suddenly SIMONE throws herself onto the table, head in her hands, and bursts into sobs. Everything stops.)*

MIMI. There it is, it's starting again....

MARIE. All right, what's the matter, Simone?

GISELE. He didn't sat that spitefully.

MME. LAURENCE. You see, you see what I've gotten mixed up in? "Rights"!

JEAN. I didn't say anything....

MME. LAURENCE. Oh, sure, we're not deaf.

MIMI. What's wrong, why are you still crying? You want me to go tell the monkey you aren't staying tonight; it wouldn't be any skin off my nose. *(SIMONE shakes her head "no".)*

MME. LAURENCE. *(rising)* Come sit in my place; you'll have a little more air. It's so hot today and with these winter fabrics on top of that.... *(SIMONE thanks MME. LAURENCE with her hand but doesn't move.)*

MIMI. *(in a low voice)* Have you got the curse? *(SIMONE shakes her head "no". MIMI continues, still more quietly.)* Were you thinking about your...?

SIMONE. *(still shaking her head)* I was thinking of nothing, of nothing.... I've nothing ... nothing....

MIMI. And what do you need with their pension; you can do plenty well without it. Go on.... It's not worth getting sick over.... Let 'em keep their pension, let 'em choke on it! *(SIMONE shrugs, as if to say that's not it either.)*

GISELE. It's your kids, they're still fighting, right.... Listen my good friend, when my youngsters get on my nerves I'd rather have *them* cry, not me; and believe me, last night I got home, the oldest stained her blouse — she'd just put it on — and now it needed to be washed again. "Slut", I said to her, "*you're* the one who's going to wash it again...." So of course her father took *her* side and everyone started shouting and crying. I cried all night.... I didn't close an eye.... Ah, I swear there are days.... *(GISELE begins to sniffle also.)*

MIMI. *(between her teeth, threatening GISELE with her fingers)* You shut up, huh?

GISELE. *(picking up again)* What's wrong? I don't have the right to say anything? *(She is now sobbing, pretending to blow her nose.)*

SIMONE. *(beating on the table)* But why am I crying, why am I crying? I don't even know why....

MIMI. Good; stop and laugh.

SIMONE. I can't, I can't.

MIMI. Tickle yourself under the arms! *(SIMONE still*

sobs. Silence.) Good then, cry, my friend; you'll piss less! *(SIMONE laughs under her tears.)* There, you see ... it's coming. Do you want me to tell you about the hunchbsck's tool.... It was all twisted, all crumpled; you had to touch it to make it straighten itself out... *(SIMONE shakes her head and her sobbing redoubles.)*

JEAN. *(while getting dressed)* Leave her alone; you're making her dizzy with all your nonsense.

MIMI. You, buzz off....

JEAN. If you all got together and insisted on being paid by the hour, he'd think twice before making you stay late. You've got to know how to make yourselves respected. Otherwise....

GISELE. Personally, I prefer to do piece-work....

JEAN. By the hour, you put in your hours and the rest is paid in overtime.

GISELE. You must feel less free....

MIMI. Especially you, who piss every five minutes....

GISELE. Me, I piss every five minutes?

MME. LAURENCE. That's nothing to be ashamed of ... go on....

GISELE. I'm not ashamed; I never go there, that's all....

MME. LAURENCE. It's not really a criticism....

GISELE. I don't go there, I never go there....

MIMI. Then why do you go out?

GISELE. I don't go out; it's the others who go out....

MME. LAURENCE. It's terrible; you'd think someone was accusing you of....

JEAN. *(after a brief silence)* You really have water on the brain.

MIMI. *(showing him the time)* You'd better run, darling, or you're going to be late for clocking in. *(JEAN leaves, slamming the door. To SIMONE, who continues to weep, working all the while.)* Now we're alone; you can let down your hair ... go on.... *(SIMONE sobs.)*

MARIE. She's going to end up choking herself.

GISELE. Do you want to stretch out for a bit? *(SIMONE is lifted onto a table.)*

SIMONE. *(Shakes her head, sighs a great gasp, then, between two sobs.)* Everything's going to be fine, everything's going to be fine, everything's going to be fine. *(brief silence)*

MIMI. *(to SIMONE)* Do you want me to tell you?

GISELE. Leave her in peace.

MIMI. A good healthy screw from time to time brushes away the cobwebs and chases away the blues.

GISELE. Pouah ... that's great ... she hasn't enough troubles without that as well? A man would give her more laundry, that's all; she already spends half the night washing her kids' underwear.

MIMI. And laundresses, they're for the dogs?

GISELE. She doesn't need that, I tell you.

MIMI. *(to SIMONE)* Don't listen to her.... Hey, Sunday I'll take you dancing; you'll pick up some handsome guy....

GISELE. You can be so disgusting ... really ... some days....

MARIE. MARIE. What she needs is someone who helps her, who supports her....

MIMI. *(Sings.)* Prosper yop la boum ... He's king of the asphalt.

MARIE. *(cutting her off, irritated)* No, I mean someone

who's good and hard-working.

MIMI. That's right, when it's hard it's good. When it's soft, it's not working. *(Everyone bursts out laughing.)*

MME. LAURENCE. *(to SIMONE, without laughing)* Are you feeling better?

SIMONE. *(wiping her eyes and laughing now)* I don't know what came over me. I was fine and then I felt as if I was choking....

MIMI. *(weeping with laughter)* Yes, in the long run you can choke on it....

GISELE. Oh shut up; let her talk.... Me, too, sometimes I feel like ... I feel like ... and then it won't come out. It's like ... like.... *(She searches for the words.)*

MIMI. Like what, sweetie?

GISELE. Like cotton-wool, here. *(She taps on her chest. To SIMONE.)* Isn't that right, isn't that right; like a wad of cotton-wool? *(SIMONE shrugs her shoulders as a sign of ignorance.)*

MIMI. *(to GISELE)* Yeah, but you've no reason; you're happy, you've a nice little husband, a nice little house, some nice little daughters....

GISELE. Sure, sure....

SIMONE. But it's the same with me; my kids are fine, they're doing well in school, there's work here all year, no off-seasons....

MIMI. What you miss....

GISELE. Give her some peace.

MIMI. Come dancing with me on Sunday; I'll tell my Joe that I have to go see my mother, since he can't stand her.

SIMONE. You're crazy; what would I do with the kids?

MIMI. They stick to you like leeches even on Sunday? Listen, my friend, you're not smart; send them to play soccer ... or to go camping....

GISELE. Thanks a lot ... so they'll catch cold ... thanks a lot....

SIMONE. Sunday is their day; we go to the movies....

MIMI. Every Sunday?

SIMONE. Except when the weather's good; then we go for a walk ... at the end of the afternoon we stop by to visit my father....

MARIE. Grandpapa's, every week? *(SIMONE nods "yes".)* With the children?

SIMONE. What choice do I have?

MIMI. Oh boy, what a charming day ... looking back on it you're dazzled. Then when do you get a change? *(brief silence)*

SIMONE. Here, with you.... *(MIMI looks at her a minute and then plunges back into her work. Everyone works in silence now. The alert has passed.)*

Scene 9

TO REBUILD HER LIFE

A summer evening in 1951. The windows are wide open. SI-MONE, seated in MME. LAURENCE'S place, sews on buttons. HELENE, at a table, tries to put some garments in cartons, crumpling them as little as possible. She gets irritated.

HELENE. These are going to be real rags....
SIMONE. Where are they going?
HELENE. Belgium....

(LEON enters, sits down at the table next to SIMONE and laughs for no reason.)

HELENE. Have you finished?
LEON. Guess what just happened to me?
HELENE. What?
LEON. I've got three aces, a black king, a red queen; I ask for two cards, I discard the king and queen and guess what I got?
HELENE. Two aces?

LEON. "Two aces"? One ace! There are only four aces in all; I already had three....

HELENE. What do I know? Why isn't Max doing this shipment?

LEON. *(to SIMONE)* Do you play cards?

SIMONE. I play War, with the kids....

LEON. A full hand of aces the first time in my life, and it has to be with my own machine operators.... It's finished now, if they want to play we'll play seriously; we're no longer the age where you play for buttons. Furthermore they're *my* buttons; they won't risk anything!

HELENE. Oh, I give up, I can't do it; the cartons are too small!

LEON. Leave it, leave it, I'm going to do it; I've got to do everything here, it's simple....

HELENE. Sure, sure.... Why isn't it Max?

LEON. I have the right to have my own customers without going through monsieur Max; I'm not tied to monsieur Max for life....

HELENE. You're sure that they'll pay at least?

LEON. Why wouldn't they pay?

HELENE. I'm asking, that's all....

LEON. Because I've had some unpaid bills, you're going.... *(He rises and helps HELENE do the package. SIMONE has finished her piece. She hangs it up and takes another. LEON to SIMONE:)* Any news from the children?

SIMONE. Yes, I received a card.

LEON. Everything all right?

SIMONE. Yes, thanks....

LEON. Where are they by now?

SIMONE. In the Federal Republic.

HELENE. So are you helping me or chatting?

LEON. I'm helping you and I'm chatting; I can do two things at once, I don't have two left hands like you....

HELENE. *(watching him do it for a minute)* Sure, it's not difficult like that, but you don't realize; they're going to be real rags when they arrive.... Go ahead and roll them into balls while you're at it....

LEON. They don't know how to iron in Belgium?

HELENE. Good, good, leave it, leave it; you're irritating me even more. I prefer to do it alone....

LEON. *(to SIMONE)* Federal Republic? That's Germany, isn't it?

HELENE. The air is very good there.

LEON. Yes, yes, that's what they say....

SIMONE. They're very happy.

LEON. You've warned them, at least?

HELENE. Leon, I beg you.

LEON. What, I haven't said anything?

HELENE. Exactly, don't say it.

LEON. It's awful, she knows in advance....

SIMONE. *(to HELENE)* I didn't want to send them over there and then I said to myself, after all, if the Jewish Federation is organizing it....

HELENE. You did well; the climate is very healthy....

LEON. Sure, sure....

SIMONE. The oldest wrote me that they took them by bus to visit Ravensbruck....

LEON. *(to HELENE abruptly)* But why are you doing up this carton now? You want them to stay crumpled up all night, eh?

HELENE. You told me that they have to leave tomorrow

morning at dawn.... I've purposely kept Simone....
(SIMONE has hung up the piece which she's just finished and gets ready to leave.)

LEON. I'll do it tomorrow; leave it....

HELENE. You won't have time tomorrow!...

LEON. Leave it, I tell you!

HELENE. No, I've started, I'll finish!

LEON. *(to SIMONE)* Stubborn, eh?... You're going to bed now?

SIMONE. Yes. I mean I'm going home....

LEON. You're not taking advantage of the kids being on vacation to....

HELENE. Leon!

LEON. What now?

HELENE. Will you stop?

LEON. What've I said? She's not at the age where.... Do we have to talk to her like a little girl — by hints?

SIMONE. *(She smiles.)* You know, in the evening I always have things to do in the house and then ... and then.... *(She laughs.)*

HELENE. Certainly ... certainly ... they don't realize....

LEON. Who realizes here? It's you who don't realize.... If you don't take advantage of the fact that the kids are gone to go out, to see people, make acquaintances, how do you expect to rebuild your life, huh, how?

SIMONE. I'm not interested in that at all, monsieur Leon; I'm fine as I am ... just fine....

LEON. *(peremptorily to SIMONE)* Sit down... *(He sits next to her.)* You know the Thermometre, place de la Republique — no, it's a cafe at the angle of the boulevard Voltaire or the avenue of the Republique, a big cafe — good. Every

Sunday morning there's a woman, madame Fanny, very nice woman, who busies herself with rebuilding the lives of people who.... You go there, at my suggestion, you talk to her and if she has someone, eh ... go find out, someone who sounds interesting, she introduces you.... That doesn't commit you to anything, right; if it works out, it works out; if it doesn't, good-bye and thanks. You're not obliged to buy; entrance is free.... Anyhow, you understand.... *(Silence. HELENE looks at SIMONE. SIMONE abruptly bursts out laughing. To HELENE.)* What's the matter with her, what did I say that's funny? Why stay alone when you can still make someone happy; there are so many men who have suffered and who are alone.... She's normal, isn't she; then she can live normally.... And even if she were ugly as sin; with a three-room apartment you can always find someone who's interested.... *(SIMONE laughs again.)* Good, let's pretend I didn't say anything....

SIMONE. *(calming herself)* Excuse me monsieur Leon, I've never been to the cafe Thermometre, but I *was* introduced to someone, not very long ago....

LEON. Ah, ah, you see? You see?

SIMONE. *(Laughs again.)* He even came to the apartment.

HELENE. *(Stops working on her package and runs to sit beside SIMOME also.)* But that's wonderful! Wonderful!

SIMONE. The kids made his life so impossible that he left and I've never seen him again; they were hateful to him.... *(She laughs.)* Happily, because the person who introduced him to me has since learned he was a guy already remarried, thanks to madame Fanny, and since he wasn't pleased with his new wife's apartment, he was looking for a larger one. That's why he'd asked to visit mine.... *(laughs)* You know what he said to me as he left: "It's a three-room, but a *small* three-room." ...I don't regret it, I'm not eager at all. To begin with, I think that even if I wanted to, I wouldn't be able to....

LEON. People say that.... Not all of them are jackasses; there are good men who're looking for someone....

SIMONE. The children are too big, they'd be unhappy, they're used to being the men of the house and then, you know, when I was married to my husband it was ann arranged marriage; they introduced us.... I must say I was fortunate; I never had any reason to complain, he was a good husband .... but today .... it would have to happen differently; if not, I don't think I'd be able to.... When this guy came over — I'd seen him once at the home of the person who introduced us — anyway, when he came over....

HELENE. How was he?

SIMONE. Fine. He had a slightly crooked mouth, but he wasn't so bad; he was a man who'd had misfortunes, *many* misfortunes .... it was hard not laughing out loud in front of him.... As soon as he had his back turned, all three of us would have a fit; the littlest began to imitate him, he did the whole apartment visit for us with comments.... The guy had a bit of a yiddish accent; the little one imitated him so terribly well, we laughed and laughed.... No, it's too complicated and then, you know, I'm comfortable like this. I feel free; I'm able to ... anyway ... good night.... *(She leaves.)*

HELENE. See you tommorow — good night. *(silence)*
LEON. Well at least I told her....

HELENE. You and your ideas. *(silence)*

LEON. Good, let's go to bed.

HELENE. *(pointing out the still-unwrapped package)* You'll do it tomorrow?

LEON. I'll do it tomorrow.

HELENE. You need a bigger carton....

LEON. No, I don't!

HELENE. And the letter?

LEON. Which letter?

HELENE. You know very well....

LEON. I'll do it tomorrow....

HELENE. Tomorrow you'll tell me tomorrow and still tomorrow....

LEON. I don't have paper....

HELENE. Do a draft on that and I'll re-copy it....

LEON. Have you got a pencil? *(HELENE gives him a pencil. He reflects a minute and then:)* What should I say?

HELENE. Please, we've talked and talked about it....

LEON. What do I say to begin? What do they use?

HELENE. "Dear cousins".

LEON. "My dear cousins".

HELENE. If you want....

LEON. "My dear cousins and children of my cousins."

HELENE. Go on; I'll take care of that part of it.

LEON. You want to write it?

HELENE. No, it's your cousin; you write....

LEON. My cousin, it's not even a real cousin, it's a distant cousin and her, I don't know her; I've never seen her. Him already I must have seen two times in my life at the absolute maximum and I was a kid; I can't even remember what he looks like, so.... *(HELENE sighs without responding.)* Good! "Dear distant cousins" or "Dear distant cousins and distant children of my distant cousins." *(He writes it down.)* There! Next?

HELENE. *(dictating)* If you are still planning to come—

LEON. Ts, ts, ts .... not so quick.... Don't you think that we ought to warn them that things are tough here as well — very tough — and that it's necessary to work? I don't know .... what do they hope for; why are they leaving there?

HELENE. We're not going over all that again; they're leaving because they can't stand living there anymore....

LEON. *(nodding agreement)* They can no longer stand it... and that, that's a serious enough reason for leaving everything and depositing yourself in a strange country with people you barely know?

HELENE. You don't want them to come? It's simple: you write that you can't receive them, period, that's all. But don't drive me crazy; we've already talked and talked it over, if you please!

LEON. I'm asking if we shouldn't warn them, that's all, that things will be tough here, too; that it's necessary to work hard. Above all they mustn't have any illusions....

HELENE. Who has any illusions?

LEON. I don't know, maybe they think that here all you have to do is lean over to scoop up the dough?

HELENE. *(getting up)* Write what you want; I'm going to bed.

LEON. That's awful ... you're the one who tells me to write and when I start to write you go to bed.

HELENE. Good, write: "Dear cousins, you will be welcome; we are waiting for you. See you soon." Signed Helene and Leon.

LEON. If that's what you want to write, you don't need me.

HELENE. I want *you* to do the writing!

LEON. Why?

HELENE. I know you, come on....

LEON. *(a sigh)* Good. "Dear distant cousins, come; we are waiting for you—" no.... "If you are still determined to come, write to tell us when you intend to arrive so we'll be better prepared to house you during the beginning of your stay." ...There, it's good like that? *(HELENE doesn't answer.)* You don't like "the beginning of your stay"?

HELENE. It's simple: if you don't want them to come, write "don't come".... I've got a headache....

LEON. I could write "don't come" to my own cousin who asks for help after all they've suffered? I simply wish that ... we have a responsibility, right? Do I know what they have in their heads, why they want to leave Poland, why they want to come here, precisely here? I don't know why they don't go to Israel, for example.... Maybe they imagine that I've an immense factory, that I'm rolling in gold and diamonds....

HELENE. *(beside herself)* They're communists; they don't give a damn for gold, they don't give a damn for diamonds. They have no one in Israel, their children speak French; they want to come to France, to live in France, to work in France!

LEON. If they're communists, why don't they stay over there where everyone is communist these days?

HELENE. Good, I'm going to bed.

LEON. Can't we discuss anything anymore? I'm trying to—

HELENE. *(cutting him off)* Discuss with the walls; me, I'm tired, I've got a headache. It's your family, you do what you want, you write them what you want.... *(LEON nods agreement. HELENE goes out crying.)*

LEON. It's awful; what did I say, what did I say? Is it my fault, is it my fault if the whole world is shit?

Scene 10

MAX

An end of an afternoon in 1952. Everyone is at work; only SIMONE is missing. There is a pile of jackets at her stool. MIMI hums. LEON enters panic-stricken and running as if he were pursued. He hurries to hide under the pressing table, behind a pile of unironed jackets, while the voice of HELENE is heard coming from the corridor.

HELENE. But since I tell you he's not here....

MAX. Where is he then, where is he?

HELENE. How would I know; we're not hooked together....

MAX. I want my merchandise, you understand, I want my merchandise; I'm not going away without my merchandise.

HELENE. As soon as it's ready....

MAX. I know, I know; you'll put it all in a taxi.... *(MAX has entered followed by HELENE who tries to calm him. MAX is at his wits' end; for an instant he contemplates the workroom with a haggard air, then, discovering the pile of pieces waiting to be finished by SIMONE, he groans.)* But nothing is ready — nothing....

HELENE. *(smiling)* You see, monsieur Max, everything which is ready has already been delivered to you.

MAX. *(shouting, piling the pieces on the floor or even tearing them from the girls' hands)* Only 40's, only 40's, I need all sizes, you've delivered only 40's, that does me no good, only 40's. *(MAX continues to gather up the pieces and put them down further on. He moves the pile under the pressing table and discovers LEON.)* Leon!

LEON. *(as if waking up)* Huh?

MAX. You're hiding under the table now!

LEON. Me, I'm hiding?

MAX. Why haven't I received—

LEON. *(emerging)* Who's hiding here? Why would I hide at home in my own house...? I've hidden enough in my life.... Thanks ... that's terrific ... so I no longer have the right to come and go under my own pressing table?

MAX. *(controlling himself)* Leon, Leon, Leon. Why'd you tell me on the phone this morning that you'd put the rest of my merchandise in a taxi and that it was going to arrive at any minute?

LEON. *(shouts)* Me, I said that? I said whatever it was on the telephone? I have the time to answer the phone?

MAX. Not you, your wife.

LEON. *(pained)* Helene, why do you say such things? *(HELENE looks at LEON without saying anything.)* Good, let's not talk about it any longer.

MAX. I have customers who are waiting for their merchandise; I've got to know, I've kept them waiting since last month — last month! This morning there was one who came into my place, sat down on a folding chair and didn't want to budge without the rest of his order.

HELENE. Surely we're not going to start waiting in each other's places of business! Soon we won't be able to work....

MAX. Madame, he in his shop, he also has customers who wait, whether it's for a marriage or for a burial.... You can't make people wait indefinitely. When you promise delivery on a certain date, it's necessary to hold to it, otherwise.... Leon, do something; we've always worked hand-in-hand, right?

LEON. Yes, but it's always *my* hand doing the work!

MAX. I swear to you that if you don't deliver everything owed to me this evening, you understand, everything, it's finished between us, finished!

LEON. It's finished? Good, then, it's finished; what should I do now; weep, hang myself?

MAX. *(with a hand on his midsection)* Leon, if one day I get an ulcer....

LEON. *(cutting him off)* An ulcer — he talks about *an* ulcer. I already have two, two and gastritis.

MAX. Good, it's finished; I can stand everything, everything, except bad faith!

LEON. *(to HELENE)* Where is the bad faith? I'm not sicker than he is, maybe?

MAX. If you'd get organized a little, instead of working like a Jew.

LEON. Ah! I see what he's up to; he wants to stick us with an Aryan production manager. With pleasure, let him come; I'm leaving him the keys and this time *I'm* heading for the Free Zone on the Riviera....

MARIE. Why did I have all 40's?

LEON. *(cutting him off)* At my place it's like that: all or nothing!

MAX. *(continuing)* It does me no good — all 40's — that's not usable. If I don't have a little of each size I can't deliver, I can't....

LEON. Do you think I keep your merchandise at my place to be perverse, huh? To deliver, to deliver — what other goal do I have in life, what other do I have?

HELENE. Leon, I beg you.... *(to MAX)* We're going to do the maximum, don't worry....

LEON. "The Maximum"! Look, look! *(He points to the workers.)* All the deprived, all the neurotic, all the unstable and even the revolutionaries come to plant their buttocks on my chairs and pretend to work; all of them have a brother, a father, a mother, a sister, children, a husband, and by turns that one gives birth, this one dies, that one gets sick. What can I do, eh, what can I do?

MAX. And at my place no one dies; no one is born at my place? I'm missing two warehousemen and my book-keeper wants to become a singer; he practices in my own office, he drives me crazy and, me, I've got to deliver piece-by-piece, chase after merchandise which you give me with a medicine dropper, keep the books, make out the bills, the out-of-town consignments.

LEON. Sure, sure, but at least you sleep at night....

MAX. *(irritated)* Me, I sleep at night? Me, I sleep at night?

LEON. As soon as I close my eyes, that one *(He indicates HELENE.)* jabs me with her elbow; "Are you asleep?" Definitely not, and that does it, she's off: Do you remember this one and that one ... it so happens they're all dead and you know how; she talks to me about them and then afterwards she weeps. She weeps and then she goes to sleep, but for me it's finished, finished, I can't sleep any longer; I get up, I go into the kitchen and I shout.... I don't want to have anything to do with the dead; the dead are dead, right, and ours are a thousand times more dead than any others because there's nothing left of them ... fine.... You've got to think of the living, and by chance the only surviving relative left to her is me, me. And she kills me at night while the others murder me during the day.... *(brief silence)*

MAX. What's that got to do with my merchandise?

LEON. Who's talking about merchandise here, who?

HELENE. Leon, I beg you.... *(MAX, a hand on his stomach, abruptly bends over in misery.)*

LEON. Look at him, look at him, my word, he wants to hit me over the head with his ulcer but if I had only ulcers, I'd go dancing every night in the jazz clubs....

MAX. Leon, seriously, let's speak man-to-man.

LEON. That's right, let's talk: what is your fabric in fact, huh? Special, pure chemical synthetic; that's what you wanted in order to make things more chic, right? You think I don't know where it comes from?

MAX. It comes from Switzerland!

LEON. That's right, that's right; it goes *through* Switzerland, it *crosses* Switzerland....

MAX. *(to HELENE)* What's he trying to say?

LEON. I said to myself, at least with Germans, we'll get deliveries on time; never a train, never a convoy late — the best shippers in the world! Only for us, you and me, monsieur Max, the fabric is late. So what? I don't say anything, I don't get upset; above all don't get upset with those guys.... And when their magical pure chemical fabric arrives, once cut, once mounted, it has a life of its own: it does what it wants, ask them.... *(The workers make some timid gestures as to the problems with the material.)* Put the iron on it, put it on. Dry: it hardens like a plank and shrinks in width. Moist: it shrinks in length and becomes as supple and agreeable as a sponge. You hang it up: it stretches, it pouches, it gets shiny, but tell him, tell him....

JEAN. It's drek!

LEON. And me, I have to watch all that and organize!

MAX. *(shouting like a madman)* Fifty percent natural fiber, fifty percent nylon, the last word in modern technique, the last word!

LEON. *(in a mutter)* Yes, yes, the last word; what is it that they have in stock over there, tons and tons? Ashes and hair, yes monsieur, don't bother shrugging your shoulders; hair, mountains of hair....

MAX. But what's he saying, what's he saying? *(LEON suddenly tears the clothes from the workers' hands and throws them at MAX'S feet, then he atacks the hanging clothing. HELENE and JEAN try to hold him back. MAX, maddened, gathers up the clothes and refolds them, muttering some incomprehensible words.)*

(A CHILD appears in the doorway. He's between ten and twelve years old, wears glasses, is only slightly astonished to discover the workroom, now in absolute disorder.)

MIMI. *(Seeing the child, calls to him.)* Come in, it's okay ... come in....

CHILD. *(Plants himself in front of LEON and then in one breath:)* My mother says to tell you she's sorry but she won't be able to come to work today....

LEON. *(shouting like a madman)* You wait until five o'clock in the evening to come and tell me that?

CHILD. *(not at all impressed)* I couldn't come before. I was at the hospital.

LEON. And your brother?

CHILD. He was at the hospital, too.

LEON. Oh wonderful; you're both sick together now, bravo!

CHILD. No, it's mother.

MIMI. She's in the hospital?

CHILD. Yes.

HELENE. What's wrong with her?

CHILD. She can't stand up; she got up to go to work this morning but she couldn't manage it, then my brother went to look for a doctor and he said that they would have to send her to the hospital. At the hospital, they said they were going to keep her under observation.

LEON. *(to MAX)* "Under observations"; you see, you see, what can I do, what can I do?

MAX. That's right, I'm going to tell my customers to tell their customers that thay won't have their clothes for getting married or going to the ball because one of your workers is in the hospital under observation.

LEON. *(shouting at HELENE)* What are you waiting for? Telephone, place an ad: "Seeking qualified finish-worker without family, without child, neither widowed, nor married, nor divorced, not mixed up in politics and in good health...." There, perhaps one time — who knows — I'll get a good hand.... And you, what're you doing clustered like flies around this kid? You're here to work, yes or shit, then work, work. But look at them, look at them, my Lord

you'd think that I was already paying them by the hour....
(HELENE has gone out.)

MAX. Leon, seriously....

LEON. Shh, we shouldn't talk in front of.... *(He indicates the workroom with his chin.)* No one is to leave this workroom until monsieur Max's order is ready for delivery. *(to JEAN)* Meeting or no meeting.... *(He has gone out. MAX and LEON can be heard arguing, then laughing. The women crowd around the CHILD. They pose a lot of questions about SIMONE'S health.)*

MARIE. What's wrong with your mother?

CHILD. *(Shrugs, then says:)* I don't know, she's tired....

MIMI. How are you and your brother going to get along?

CHILD. Doing what?

MIMI. Eating and all that.

CHILD. Oh! We're going to find a way; I know how to cook and at noon nothing's changed; we eat at the school.

JEAN. The hospital, it's Lariboisiere?

CHILD. No, I put the name of the hospital and all that on a piece of paper; it's in the suburbs.... *(MIMI takes the paper.)*

GISELE. You kill yourself raising kids....

MARIE. You've got to love her very much, your mother....

MIMI. Always.

MME. LAURENCE. You're nice to her at least?

JEAN. Leave him be....

GISELE. That's a beautiful coat; is it the one the Americans sent you?

CHILD. I don't like it ... it's a girl's coat.

GISELE. They're still very nice, the Americans, to send coats to young French children....

CHILD. I don't like the Americans.

GISELE. Why not, my rabbit?

CHILD. I'm not a rabbit, I like the Russians, the Americans want war....

JEAN. Bravo ... for your trouble I'm going to give you a piece of candy....

CHILD. I don't like candy, thanks, I've got to go....

MIMI. Tell your mother to come back quickly; that we'll go to see her and ... can you give us a good-bye kiss or are you already too grown-up a monsieur to kiss the ladies? *(The CHILD comes back, he hugs MIMI; MIMI slips a bill into his hand; the CHILD refuses it.)* Yes, yes, you're to buy something for yourself and for your brother, too. *(The others also embrace him.)*

GISELE. What does she complain of, your mother?

CHILD. She doesn't complain; she just can't stay on her feet.

GISELE. Does she still cry as much?

CHILD. Maman? She never cries....

MME. LAURENCE. She'll soon be well enough to come back to work....

CHILD. *(kissing MME. LAURENCE)* Later, my brother and I, we'll work and she'll never have to work again. *(They all approve. The CHILD starts to leave.)*

JEAN. What about me; you don't kiss me!

CHILD. Men don't kiss. *(Everyone works.)*

GISELE. *(Sings "The White Roses" mechanically.)*

TODAY IS SUNDAY MORNING

THESE ARE FOR YOU, MAMAN
I BROUGHT YOU WHITE ROSES
FOR YOU LOVE THEM SO
NOW THAT YOU'VE GONE AWAY
TO THAT GARDEN ABOVE—

    MIMI. *(cutting her off)* Shut up.... *(GISELE stops singing. The work continues for a moment in silence.)*

FIN

TIME OF YEAR BREAKDOWN

Scene 1	THE TRY-OUT	1945, Autumn, Early Morning, start of the day
Scene 2	SONGS	1946, Winter, Late Morning, before lunch
Scene 3	NATURAL SELECTION	1946, Autumn, End of the Work Day
Scene 4	THE PARTY	1947, Spring, Late Afternoon
Scene 5	NIGHT	1947, Autumn, Night
Scene 6	THE COMPETITION	1948, Spring, Before Noon
Scene 7	THE DEATH CERTIFICATE	1949, Winter, Afternoon, after lunch
Scene 8	THE MEETING	1950, Summer, 5:30 in the Evening
Scene 9	TO REBUILD HER LIFE	1951, Summer, Evening
Scene 10	MAX	1952, Winter, Late Afternoon

There is one intermission.
It occurs after Scene 5.

HOW THE WORKROOM FUNCTIONS

Each woman works on a separate part of the jacket. Each jacket is worked on in a specific order. All of the work performed by these women is part of the finishing work on a suit.

The jobs they do and the order in which they are done:
1. Gisele — pins and bastes the shoulder pads into the jackets.
2. Mimi — hand sews each of the buttonholes.
3. Marie — sews the buttons on.
4. Mme. Laurence — sews the sleeve lining into the shoulder. It has been partially pinned in place when she is given the jacket.
5. Simone — does all the hemming on the jacket.

Each job requires a different sewing stitch and allows for its own short cuts.

Helene acts as a foreman to the room. She oversees everything that is being worked on. She begins by tagging each one of the garments. Depending on what is needed to be accomplished on the suit, she gives it to the specific worker who does that task. After the seamstress has finished her specific work on the jacket, she rips off the tag, puts it in her box (at the end of the week she is payed per tag) and goes on to the next jacket that Helene has layed out for her. As the women complete their assigned tasks, Helene gathers them up, inspects them, re-tags them and lays them out for the next lady to work on. Each coat continues this same path until it is completely finished. The ladies *never* hand the garment to the next worker themselves. That is only done by Helene.

For the workers there is a hierarchy within the workroom. Mme. Laurence is the "queen bee"; not only because she is the oldest and has been there the longest, but because of her specific job. She sews the sleeve lining into the shoulder of the jacket. It requires great skill as well as a rudimentary understanding of cutting. Without this understanding she could set the sleeve lining into the garment incorrectly. Mimi is the next in line. Her skill of sewing buttonholes by hand requires great patience and immense concentration. The animosity between these two women stems not only from personality conflicts, but also from the natural feelings of two rivals for the top position. Further down the hierarchial line, and the next woman to join the workroom, is Gisele. Her job of setting the shoulder pads into the suit, though requiring less skill than either Mme. Laurence or Mimi's jobs, still requires an understanding and knowledge of the working of the garment or the coat will not hang properly when worn. These are highly skilled workers. They have little fear of being fired. With such skills as they possess they could easily find jobs elsewhere. Marie, the youngest of the women, is still an apprentice of sorts when the play begins (hence the lowly job of sewing buttons on). Simone does the fine hand-stitching of the hems (bottom of the jacket and sleeves). She probably does not work as fast as the other women but takes great care and pride in her work. Since she is the last one to join the workroom she is no threat to anyone, therefore everyone takes a liking to her and tries to help her.

Now to the Presser — the garments when they are totally finished are given to him for the final pressing into shape. The suits would have been pressed at different stages of their development; whether by this Presser or another, that is not clear in the script. The irons he works with are the old heavy, metal irons. They are put on a gas heater to heat up. When they are hot enough, he takes the iron pressers hook from the wall (it looks similar to an "S" with one of the curved ends much smaller than the other), loops it around the handle of the hot iron, scoops it up off the gas burner, dunks it in a bucket of water (so it won't scorch the material) and puts it on the iron resting plate. He covers the suit with a damp cloth and then with an asbestos pot holder of sorts he lifts the hot iron and begins his work. He does not glide the iron as we do our steam and dry irons of today, but constantly keeps picking it up and putting it down with pressure. They often used a wood block as well to literally pound the material into shape (hence the pounding the script asks for).

It was not an easy task to reconstruct the way a workroom of this period functioned. People who lived during this period are understandably very hesitant to be questioned about it. It took many hours of research and depending on what source you used the answers could differ quite a bit. But with the help of several tailoring experts, books, photographs, etc. and with the guidelines set down in Mr. Grumberg's play, this is the way we believe the workroom functioned in that time and place. However, having not lived in that time, I cannot in all honesty swear to the full accuracy of all that I have set down.

PROPERTY PLOT

5 sewing boxes
Sewing needles
Straight pins
Safety pins
6 thimbles
6 pin cushions
6 scissors
1 fabric shears
2 tape measures
Spools of thread
Bee's wax
Buttons
Pencils
Tags (for suits)
1 compact
2 lipstick
1 tin of cough drops
1 aspirin tin
5 combs
5 handkerchiefs
Cigarettes
4 lunch pails
2 spoons
2 napkins
2 placemats
Food (cheese, bread, etc.)
1 drinking glass
French coins (20 Sous)
French Francs
Boxes for buttons (on table)

Boxes for straight pins (on table)
Boxes for safety pins (on table)
Jar for pencils (on table)
2 metal buckets
2 pressing irons
1 pressing iron stand
1 pressing iron hook
1 asbestos pot holder
1 pressing ham
2 cloths (for Presser)
Gas stove with two burners (Electric hot plate under it)
Record player
3 "78" records
1 gift-wrapped box
1 woman's sheer night gown
2 wine bottles with corks
1 cork screw
1 tablecloth
11 assorted wine glasses
3 World War II gasoline lamps
1 tray
1 liquor bottle
1 note (pinned to the back of a jacket
   saying "THIS IS SEWING FOR THE DEAD")
1 French govt. document and envelope (death certificate)
Brown paper (for tables)
3 cartons
Tissue paper
2 pieces of candy
1 note for the Boy
Suit jackets
Wooden hangers

PROPERTIES PLOT

SET PIECES:
Sewing table with drawers
Five 24-inch stools
Small table
Cutting table
Sewing machine table
Presser's table
Iron table
One 18-inch stool
Thread trunk
3 sawhorses
Waste basket
Chair
Footstool
Wash basin
Table by sink

SET DRESSING:
Iron
Candle
Mixed buttons
6 pin cushions
Wall phone
Dust pan
Sewing ham
Gasoline lamp
2 calendars
6 spools of thread
Misc. snippets of cloth
Push broom
Several ashtrays

SCENE 1:
Tin of cough drops

SCENE 2:
Two coins
Container of buttons
5 glasses
Bottle of aspirin
4 lunch boxes with food
Cigarettes
Matches

SCENE 4:
10 glasses
2 champagne bottles
Record player
3 "78" Records
Gift box
Comb
2 sets of make-up
5 thimbles
Plate of cheese with knife
Plate of bread
Tablecloth

SCENE 5:
Matches
Tray
Teapot
Liter of Eau-de-vie
3 glasses
Sportcoat
Cup of coffee

SCENE 6:
Baggy jacket
Note on jacket ("This is sewing for the dead.")
2 handkerchiefs

SCENE 7:
Envelope
Death certificate
Cutting shears

SCENE 8:
Suit box
3 workers almanacs

SCENE 9:
Pencil
Piece of paper

SCENE 10:
Paper money
Piece of candy

PERSONAL PROPS

Simone's sewing box with scissors, bees wax, needles,
    thimble, thread.
Gisele's sewing box with the same.
Marie's sewing box with the same.
Mimi's sewing box with the same.
Mme. Laurence's sewing box with the same.

COSTUME PLOT

SIMONE:
1. Blouse, Skirt, Slip, Seamed hose, Coat, Sewing smock, Purse
2. Blouse, Skirt, Purse

GISELE:
1. Dress, Smock, Slip, Hose, Coat, Purse
2. Dress (party)
3. Dress

MARIE:
1. Dress, Slip, Seamed hose, Coat, Purse
2. Dress (party)
3. Pregnant padding, Dress, Slip, Slippers
4. Sleevless dress, Smock

MME. LAURENCE:
1. Dress, Slip, Seamed hose, Pearls, Glasses, Coat, Hat, Gloves, Smock
2. Blue suit
3. Green dress

MIMI:
1. Skirt, Sweater, Belt, Slip, Seamed hose, Coat, Purse, Glasses, Man's shirt for smock
2. Blouse, Jacket

HELENE:
1. Overdress, Skirt, Seamed hose, Slip, Jewelry
2. Dress
3. Robe, Slippers
4. Dress
5. Blouse, Skirt, Jacket

LEON:
1. Suit, Shirt, Tie, Socks
2. Sweater, Pants
3. Vest
4. Tailor's apron

FIRST PRESSER:
1. Pants, Short-sleeved work shirt, Jacket, Belt, Work shoes

SECOND PRESSER:
1. Pants, Work shirt, Jacket

FIRST MACHINE OPERATOR:
1. Two-piece suit, Shirt, Tie

SECOND MACHINE OPERATOR:
1. Pants, Coat, Shirt, Tie

MAX:
1. Two-piece suit, Shirt, Tie, Hat

BOY:
1. Shorts, T-shirt, Sweater, Coat, Knee socks, Hat

SOUND PLOT

SOUND 1 . . . . White Roses (with vocals)

SOUND 2 . . . . Tango (in Yiddish)

SOUND 3 . . . . Waltz (in Yiddish)

SOUND 4 . . . . Tag

SOUND 5 . . . . White Roses (instrumental)

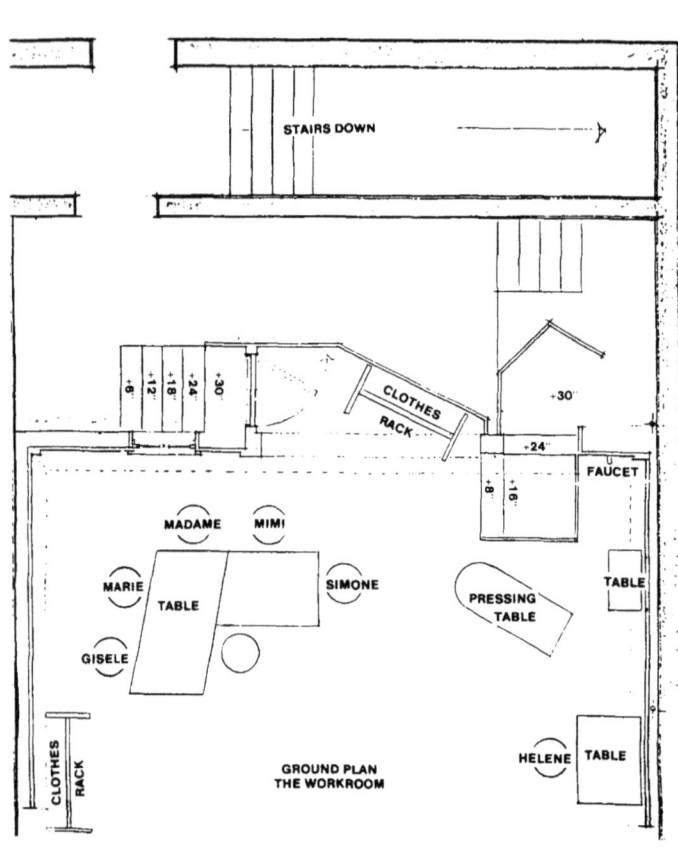

STAIRS DOWN

CLOTHES RACK

+30'

+24"

FAUCET

+8'

+16'

+6'

+12'

+18'

+24'

+30'

MADAME   MIMI

MARIE

TABLE

SIMONE

PRESSING
TABLE

TABLE

GISELE

CLOTHES RACK

HELENE   TABLE

GROUND PLAN
THE WORKROOM

HISTORICAL BACKGROUND

World War II devastated the face of Europe in a way which is difficult for those who were not there to understand. We can only try to imagine what it is like to live in a world torn to shreds. The post-war years of reconstruction reflected this devastation. When the war was finally over and the shouts of victory faded, the survivors were left to salvage what they could of their lives. But perhaps the hardest part was letting go of what could not be salvaged and moving on. *The Workroom* is a portrait of the survivors.

DRANCY: French town, chief transit camp for Auschwitz. "... an enormous, half-finished apartment complex in a suburb northeast of Paris served as an ante-chamber to Auschwitz.... All but 12 of the 79 deportation trains carrying Jews to the east left from Drancy, as did over 67,000 of the close to 75,000 Jews deported from French soil. Regular departures began in the summer of 1942 and continued until 31 July 1944. About 70,-000 Jews passed through its gates — and, except for a very few, this was the last they saw of France."

from *Vichy France and the Jews* by Marrus and Paxton

LUBLIN-MAIDANEK: outside of Lublin in southeast

Poland, Maidanek was one of the four major concentration camps.

RAVENSBRUCK: German concentration camp located 20-30 miles north of Berlin, used exclusively for the detention and extermination of women.

FREE ZONE: unoccupied portion of France after defeat by Germans. Vichy France (southwest), ostensibly free of German control.

VICHY GOVERNMENT: named after the French town of Vichy where the regime was established in 1940. Fascist and anti-semitic, the Vichy Government controlled France until '44 when Allied forces along with French Resistance liberated the country and Charles DeGaulle returned as President of the Provisional government.

"It is striking with what alacrity the Vichy regime ... deliberately adopted an anti-Jewish policy after the defeat of 1940... We can find no trace of German attempts to extend their own anti-Jewish policy to the Unoccupied Zone in the summer of 1940... Vichy anti-Jewish policy was thus not only autonomous from German policy; it was a rival to it..."

"When the Germans began their systematic deportation and extermination of Jews in 1942, Vichy's rival anti-semitism offered them more substantial help than they received anywhere else in western Europe..."

"The most vulnerable by far, of course, were those who were most unwelcome in France, the refugees from Germany and eastern Europe for whom no one would speak any more; among the last category the poorest were most vulnerable..."

from *Vichy France and the Jews* by Marrus and Paxton

The scenes of *The Workroom* occur between 1945 and 1952. Between '45 and '47 the provisional post-war government of France became the Fourth Republic and the country, in only 3 years, passed through the hands of 3 presidents. The reeling economy was bolstered by American dollars and by the nationalization of major banks and industries, but the shortage of food and materials necessitated the continuance of extreme rationing and insured the proliferation of black market business. Having survived the war, the population of France, of the world, had to struggle desperately for a personal peace.